"The 99-year-old female narrator o.⸺⸺⸺⸺ spins a wickedly engaging and hilarious yarn as she unloads her secrets. The story crackles with snappy dialogue, sorcery, romantic and evil spells, a mummy, oracles, jettatores, explosions, disembodied limbs, and boozy parties set in Italian olive groves. This reader didn't want this party of a novel to end! Melissa Hardy practices her own kind of wizardry as her entertaining troupe of unusual characters navigates through humorous and imaginative terrains. One of the funniest novels I've read in a long time—maybe ever."

—CATHARINE LEGGETT, author of
The Way to Go Home and *In Progress*

"I had been under the apparently false impression that oracles are always dignified and confined to a single sacred space, but the oracle in Melissa Hardy's new novel is sly, meddlesome and peripatetic. She gets around in the company of a scruffy, independent-minded young girl, the narrator of this hilarious, anachronistic, romance/comedy of errors. Written by a self-confessed Italophile, and mostly set in early nineteenth century Italy, *The Oracle of Cumae* is a fascinating book of secrets 'steeped in tradition and marinated in superstition'"

—STAN DRAGLAND, author of
Strangers & Others: The Great Eastern

"Melissa Hardy is quietly becoming one of the best writers of short fiction working today, equally at ease with modern realist fiction, historical fiction, magical realism, and pure fantasy."

—TERRI WINDLING, editor,
The Year's Best Fantasy and Horror (2003)

THE ORACLE OF CUMAE

MELISSA HARDY

Second Story Press

Library and Archives Canada Cataloguing in Publication

Title: The oracle of Cumae / Melissa Hardy
Names: Hardy, Melissa, author.
Identifiers: Canadiana (print) 20190076313 | Canadiana (ebook) 20190076321 |
    ISBN 9781772601145 (softcover) | ISBN 9781772601152 (EPUB)
Classification: LCC PS8565.A63243 O73 2019 | DDC C813/.54—dc23

Cover by Natalie Olsen
Edited by Carolyn Jackson
Design by Melissa Kaita

Printed and bound in Canada

*Second Story Press gratefully acknowledges the support of the
Ontario Arts Council and the Canada Council for the Arts for our
publishing program. We acknowledge the financial support of the
Government of Canada through the Canada Book Fund.*

ONTARIO ARTS COUNCIL
CONSEIL DES ARTS DE L'ONTARIO
an Ontario government agency
un organisme du gouvernement de l'Ontario

Canada Council   Conseil des Arts
for the Arts   du Canada

Funded by the Government of Canada
Financé par le gouvernement du Canada

Canadä

Published by
SECOND STORY PRESS
20 Maud Street, Suite 401
Toronto, ON M5V 2M5
www.secondstorypress.ca

MIX
Paper from
responsible sources
FSC
www.fsc.org   FSC® C004071

*This book is dedicated to
my granddaughter, Victoria.
May you be fierce.*

PROLOGUE

THE MORNING that Mariuccia Umbellino turned ninety-nine, she asked her great-great-nephew, Cesare Bacigalupo V, otherwise known as Cico, to fetch her a priest. "There is something I want to tell him," she said. "A terrible secret." Then, as he was turning to go, she grabbed hold of his shirt-sleeve. "And Cico, don't you be fetching me that old fool Eusebio! No! Wait a minute!" She held up a hand. It resembled nothing so much as a fallen leaf, brittle and curled about the edges, and so paper thin as to be transparent. She bowed her head and, squeezing her eyes closed, mentally hacked her way back through the thick tangle of eighty-odd years to arrive at the point where she remembered what had happened to Eusebio. "Ah, yes!" She settled back into the battered India reed wheelchair and smiled, showing a remarkable number of

1

teeth for a woman her age. "Eusebio choked on a biscuit. A greedy, selfish little man. In the end, it did him in." Catching Cico's confused look, she laughed. "Don't worry. All this would have taken place before you were born." But was that true, she wondered. It was difficult to know for certain exactly which Cesare Cico was. There had been so many, each bearing a strong resemblance to the first of that name—her long deceased brother-in-law—paunchy, with black mustachios, red lips, and ridiculously small feet. When she lost focus, when she did not concentrate, they all tended to blend together in her mind, the five Cesare Bacigalupi whom she had known over the course of her long lifetime.

As for Cico, he was astonished. His beloved and terrifying auntie had not attended Mass for more than eighty years and had committed this sin of omission with a degree of tart defiance that had puzzled and alarmed her family for generations.

"Aren't you afraid you will go to Hell?" they would ask her.

"I have no intention of going to Hell," she would reply. "And if St. Peter won't let me through the Pearly Gates, why, then, I shall go to the Elysian Fields."

So it was with great excitement that Cico Bacigalupo bounced down the stairs two at a time, ripped his hat from the rack, threw open the heavy oak door, and burst onto the Piazza Libertà. The month was April and the hour early enough that the cobblestones were still slick with chilly dew. Crossing the piazza, he headed east on the narrow, dark Via Ugolino until he reached the portico of the convent of San Francesco, the bell of which he proceeded to ring with an impatience that bespoke his errand's urgent nature.

After a few moments, a Poor Clare opened the door. The nun was barefoot and black-veiled, her blue serge habit tied around the waist with a white cord, knotted four times to symbolize the vows she had taken—obedience, poverty, virginal chastity, and enclosure. "Signor Bacigalupo!" she greeted him, for his was a familiar face—he was, after all, a prominent businessman from a prominent family. "What is your business with us this fine morning?"

"Ah, Sister Benedetta!" Cico beamed, beside himself with joy. "I must see Padre Bernardino at once! A miracle has occurred, and, if we do not seize the day, I fear a golden opportunity may pass! *My auntie wishes to speak with a priest!*"

"*Addio!*" Sister Benedetta clapped her hand over her heart. "Signorina Umbellino? You mean she must want to confess? A miracle, indeed! Please come in, Signor." Opening the door wider, she ushered him into a gallery that opened onto a courtyard, pointed to a marble bench, and bustled off, her bare feet padding across the tile floor.

A moment later she returned, the convent's reluctant pastor in tow. Padre Bernardino was a slight, melancholy man with a woebegone expression and hairy ears. He had reason to be melancholy. Although the Bishop had appointed him shepherd to this flock of cloistered women, their roles had somehow become reversed. By constant bullying, nagging, mothering, and smothering the nuns ruled over the priest and not the other way around. "Stand up straight, Padre," Sister Benedetta scolded him now. "And look here! *Tch, tch!* Food stains! What will Signorina Umbellino think? She will think we don't take good care of you." Removing a linen handkerchief from her sleeve, she spat on it and dabbed furiously at the front of his cassock. "There! Now you'll do. But only just." She turned to Cico. "Do you believe it? This rascal was trying to hide from me! Say hello to Signor Bacigalupo, Father. Go on, now."

Bernardino made a sour face at the nun before turning to Cico and extending a damp, limp hand for him to shake. "Signor," he greeted the businessman without enthusiasm. "I understand that your aunt wishes to speak to a priest."

"My great-great-aunt," Cico clarified. "That is correct, Father, but we must hurry, for she might change her mind, and that would be too bad."

The two men bade farewell to Sister Benedetta and made their way up the narrow Via Ugolino and across the Piazza Libertà toward the Casa Bacigalupo. This was an imposing three-story structure, built in the seventeenth century around a central courtyard, with thick, apricot-colored walls and green louvered windows. Overlooking the piazza was an ornate wrought-iron balcony, lined with terra-cotta planters filled with red geraniums. On this same balcony a wheelchair had been parked. In it sat an old woman, no bigger than a girl and wrapped in a red shawl.

Bernardino stopped in his tracks. "Is that *her*?" he whispered. Although he had heard a great deal about the famous, indeed, one might go so far as to say *infamous* Mariuccia Umbellino, he had never seen her. He came from Pontericcioli, a small town to the south and east of Casteldurante, and had been dispatched to minister to the Poor Clares only a decade before; the old woman had ceased to venture forth some fifteen years before that.

"It is!" Cico replied fondly. For a reason Bernardino was

about to discover, the Bacigalupo men doted on Mariuccia, who, in turn, turned up her nose at them. "Hallo, Auntie!" Cico called, waving at the old woman.

She acknowledged his greeting with a curt nod, then looked pointedly away.

Cico chuckled. "She has never been what you would call warm. Nothing soft about her. Did you know that she single-handedly ran Bacigalupo & Sons for more than fifty years? Up until ten years ago, that is, when I took over." Bacigalupo & Sons specialized in the manufacture and exportation of fine majolica ware and was the largest and most profitable such enterprise in the entire region of Alto Metauro.

"I had heard that." Bernardino clenched his teeth so they would not chatter. Women in general alarmed him. Capable women terrified him. Then there was the matter of class— Cesare Bacigalupo and his auntie were Casteldurantean aristocracy, while Bernardino was the son of a humble cheese-maker from a small backwater. Although it was early in the day, he could already smell himself—garlic and onions and just that hint of tangy cheese that was his birthright, mixed with wood smoke and the pungent odor imparted to his cassock by the cheap black dye used by the nuns in its manufacture. It was not a good combination. He wished that he could do something about it, but knew that this was hopeless.

Cico bounded up three marble steps, worn slick by two centuries of use, and flung open the front door to his ancestral home. "Come in! Come in! What a treat awaits you, Padre! You get to meet my auntie!"

Reluctantly Bernardino followed Cico into the foyer, up a narrow staircase to the house's second floor, and to the end of a gloomy corridor lined with closed doors and dark ancestral portraits.

"Don't let her eat you alive," Cico whispered. He knocked, then called out, "Auntie? Can you hear me? Here's Padre Bernardino from the convent."

"Bring him in!" Although her voice crackled with age, the old woman's tone was still commanding.

Cico opened the door to reveal a large, airy room, sparsely furnished, with a high, vaulted ceiling and a tiled floor, over which lay a red Turkish carpet. The French doors to the balcony stood open and, through them, Bernardino could see the back of the old woman's wheelchair.

"Come, Cico!" she said now. "Bring him to me. Don't dawdle. I'm ridiculously old, you know. I could die at any minute."

"Ninety-nine years young today and trust me when I say she doesn't look a day over seventy!" Taking hold of the priest's arm, Cico steered him out onto the balcony and made the introductions. "Auntie, this is Father Bernardino from the convent of San Francesco. Padre, my adorable great-great-aunt, Signorina Mariuccia Umbellino."

Clearly 'adorable' was in the eye of the beholder, for it occurred to Bernardino now that Mariuccia Umbellino bore the same degree of resemblance to a woman that a raisin bears to a grape—as if she had somehow imploded. All of her features, except for a pair of keen, dark eyes, were encased in wrinkles. She was no taller than a twelve-year-old child and could not have weighed more than eighty pounds. What's more, if he was not mistaken, she wore a man's trousers under the robe that lay across her lap and, beneath the shawl wrapped around her shoulders, a man's jacket, cut in a fashion popular several decades earlier. So it was true, he thought, what he had heard, that Mariuccia Umbellino was more like a man than a woman.

"Charmed, I'm sure," mumbled Bernardino and awkwardly thrust out his hand in greeting, hoping that it would not prove distastefully sweaty. When the old woman showed no inclination to take it, Bernardino quickly and somewhat gratefully withdrew it and thrust it deep into one of the side pockets sewn into his cassock.

"Charmed?" Her tone was arch. "Surely not, Padre! I am a very old person, skin riding bones. There's nothing charming about me!"

"On the contrary!" Cico protested adoringly.

"Still here, Cico?" She sounded exasperated. "Fetch this young man a chair and go away. What I am going to tell him is not for your ears. Oh, now, don't look so disappointed! You didn't think that you would get to know my terrible secret, did you? Close the door on your way out and, Cico, no listening through the keyhole!"

Cico looked offended. He drew himself up to his full height and thrust out his chest. "I am not a child, Auntie," he informed her loftily. "In any case, I have a business that requires seeing to."

"The business that I preserved and built upon for fifty years so that it might be yours!" she reminded him.

Clearly Cico could not stay angry at her long. He chuckled. "I warn you, Padre, though she is lovely as a rose, her thorns are sharp." He exited the balcony, returning a moment later with a chair that he placed opposite the old woman's wheelchair so that Bernardino might sit facing her with his back to the piazza. Then he planted a kiss on a little bald spot on the top of his great-great-auntie's head. "I wish you a good confession, Auntie," he said and left, making a great show of pulling the French doors closed behind him.

"Confession!" muttered the old woman. "Ridiculous!" She turned her attention to the priest. "Sit down," she told him. "I hope this heat is not too much for you. I am like an old cat, always cold in the bones, always seeking the warmth of the sun."

Bernardino grunted something noncommittal. In fact, he was already uncomfortably warm, so much so that his heavy, dank cassock was beginning to stick awkwardly to his sweaty body. Inwardly he cursed the Poor Clares who had sewn this garment for him out of the cheapest, scratchiest wool they could find. Them and their infernal vow of poverty!

But Mariuccia Umbellino was addressing him. "So you replaced Padre Eusebio at the convent? The Capella Cola, as well?"

The Capella Cola, next door to the Casa Bacigalupo, was a tiny, independent chapel that served as the headquarters of the Brotherhood of Good Death, a lay confraternity that arranged for the transport and burial of deceased paupers, assisted the dying, registered the dead, and distributed money to the poor. Although the Capella Cola had no temporal connection to the Convent of San Francesco, the Poor Clares had, for centuries, loaned their priest to its handful of a congregation for the purpose of saying mass several times a week.

"Yes and no," replied Bernardino. He pulled at his Roman collar in an effort to promote air flow. "Yes, I serve as the priest of San Francesco and say Mass at the Capella, but Padre Eusebio died a very long time ago. There have been several priests since his time."

The old woman shrugged. "I wouldn't know. I haven't set foot in the Chiesa di San Francesco...or the Capella Cola... or any other church for that matter for a very, very long time. Longer, I'd wager, than you've been alive."

Bernardino cleared his throat. "Perhaps if you were to confess, you would feel that there was once again a place for you in God's house. Is there, perhaps, some sin that weighs on your conscience?"

The old woman glared at him. "Some *sin?* Don't be absurd! I have acted of necessity at times, but I have never, ever *sinned.* The matter I wish to discuss with you is something else entirely. It is a secret that I have kept since I was a girl...one I wish to disburden myself of before I die. I have kept it to myself far too long."

Cowed, Bernardino swallowed hard. "Yes, Signorina," he stammered. "Whatever you say!"

"I take it that priests are still obliged to honor the confidentiality of the confessional? That hasn't changed?"

"No, Signorina."

"Then I will tell you my secret. Well, my *secrets*, for there are several. Now. Here. That is, after all, why I sent for you."

What follows is what Mariuccia Umbellino told Padre Bernardino Franconero in confidence on her ninety-ninth birthday. It is the same story that Bernardino Franconero told Padre Giuseppe Tosti fifty-two years later on his deathbed. And it is the same story that Giuseppe Tosti, who was to leave the priesthood to marry, told his daughter, Filomena Tosti, who undertook to write it down. Signorina Tosti prefaced her account with these words: "This story I am about to relate… for the record, I don't believe a word of it. Nevertheless…"

PART ONE

IT MAY surprise you to know that I, Mariuccia Umbellino, was not a native of Casteldurante. Not many people know that. I have outlived all those who would remember where I came from and when and why. I hailed from Montemonaco—a little village strewn about the upper slopes of Monte Vettore, one of the highest peaks in the southern Sibylline Mountains, some one hundred and fifty miles to the south of here in the province of Macerata. Montemonaco was not so much a village as a loose collection of agricultural concerns—vineyards, olive groves, scrubby orchards of chestnut and hazel bushes, and various grazing operations. These were owned by perhaps as many as two dozen families, all of whom had inhabited those heights since pre-Roman times.

At the center of my village stood a small stone church dedicated to San Sebastiano. Above its humble altar hung a dark and terrifying oil painting of that saint's martyrdom.

He was shown naked, save for a strategically draped loin cloth, with his head thrown back, his mouth agape, eyes rolling and nostrils flaring, and stuck so full of arrows that he resembled a porcupine. Needless to say, we children of the parish found this painting sufficiently lurid that we never objected to attending Mass, which was, at any rate, shorter in Montemonaco than elsewhere. This was because our parish priest, Padre Antonio DiNardo, was blind and, as such, could neither read nor write and so had substituted a kind of dumb show for Mass. By this I mean that he would go through the motions of the Mass, pressing his hands together in prayer and casting his unseeing eyes upward when he wished us to pray, making the sign of the cross when he wished us to do likewise, pantomiming kneeling when it was the congregation's turn to do that, and so forth and so on.

As for my family, the Umbellini, we lived about fifteen minutes up the road from San Sebastiano, just beyond the village's edge. Ours was a rambling mud and straw farmhouse, crumbling portions of which dated back to the second century after Christ.

My father, Umberto Umbellino, tended to the ancient grove of olive trees surrounding our house, gnarled as old men, and was a renowned hunter and trapper—wolves, whose pelts were much prized, abounded in those days, as did boar and deer and martens of various sorts.

My mother, Esperanza Umbellino, kept a prize herd of goats and sold what cheese and milk the family could not eat. Of the seven children she bore my father, five survived to adulthood: in order of birth there was my elder sister Concetta, then me, then three younger brothers—Carmine,

12

Emilio, and Rinardo. These boys were rarely apart and func-tioned much like a rowdy dog pack—they were raucous in their enthusiasm and most often perceived as a blur of motion. Of all those children, I alone survive, but that is hardly sur-prising. I always was bad-tempered and bad-tempered people, I have noticed, tend to live longer.

The Umbellini were not poor. We were neither peasants nor savages. We might have been country folk and unsophis-ticated in our ways, but we were the most prosperous family in Montemonaco and had been since Roman times, which is as far back as the collective memory of my village stretched. My father's olive grove was the largest and the best produc-ing in the region. The oil we pressed was light and fruity and green. The wine we squeezed from our grapes was known for its clarity and our *mistà* for its potency—this was a brandy Papa distilled from the fermented residue of grapes pressed for winemaking.

As for my mother, her goats were famous for the sweet-ness of their milk, the creamy tartness of their cheese, and their sublime good looks—ours was the prettiest herd of goats in all the Marches and, I dare say, of neighboring Umbria as well. Our land was extensive and well situated to receive the benefits of weather, and our house, if inelegant, was large and comfortable. Our part of the mountain was generous in its gifts—cheese, bread and olives, grapes for wine, game that was always plentiful—my parents were good stewards of the land, as had been their forebears, and we had not learned to want what it could not easily give us. As for gold and sil-ver, which we sometimes required, though only occasionally, there was the annual truffle hunt. In the fall, the entire village of Montemonaco mustered dogs and pigs and spread out over the limestone mountains to hunt for truffles among the scrubby woods of white oak and manna, ash, and hornbeam. The Umbellini, having the best pigs and the best dogs, always harvested the most and the best truffles. The men would then take the autumnal harvest of succulent pale mushrooms to the valley towns below to sell at market for a price that took our breath away. To us Montemonaci, Casteldurante was just another valley town whose inhabitants did not know better than to pay ridiculously inflated prices for things that were, after all, second cousins once removed to soil, moss, and bark.

The bottom line, Padre, is this: my parents were simple people who lived the way their mothers and fathers had and their mothers and fathers before them—in harmony with the mountain, with its permission and at its pleasure, and I was raised to believe in the power of sacred things…in the utility of spells. We did not concern ourselves overly with the architecture of Heaven and Hell, nor did we unduly strain our credulity by trying to imagine how many angels might dance on the head of a pin. How could we presume to speculate on matters that are, by their very nature, unknowable? We were good Catholics, but we were also good pagans in the original sense of that word—for the word *pagan* comes from the Latin *paganus*, meaning a rustic, one who lives in the countryside, as opposed to the city.

What my fellow villagers did know for an absolute certainty was that Old Ones lived in the wild and desert places of our blue mountains—indwelling spirits, who are neither born nor are they likely to die, whom our ancestors knew as the gods and goddesses of these places. Holy Church may have reviled these Old Ones, calling them shapeshifters and sorcerers and hags. It may have sought to confine them to distant crags and remote vales to live wild alongside wolves, eagles, falcons, and orchids. But the inhabitants of our region, at least, were careful to pay them the full measure of respect due them for, like a rich landlord or a potent magistrate, they have the power to help or to hinder and are, by nature, meddlesome, fickle, and easily offended.

One of the greatest of these lived just up the road from us; she had done so for more than forty generations. I have said that the Umbellini were prosperous, that we lacked for nothing. This was not accidental: since the fourth century Anno Domini, the Umbellini had served as the gatekeepers to the Grotto delle Fate, the home of the Oracle Sibylla, she from whom our mountains took their name. This is her story.

Long, long ago, in the times before Christ, there were Oracles consulted by kings and heroes. One of the greatest of these was Sibylla, the Oracle at Cumae in Campania. According to the poet Virgil, who was very knowledgeable about such matters, it was Sibylla who showed Aeneas the way to the underworld—no small feat. As Christianity gained ground in Europe, however, Sibylla's popularity waned. Then a sixth-century bishop, wishing to capitalize on his parishioners' seeming inability to distinguish between the Son of God on the one hand and the God of the Sun on the other, caused a church to be erected over the ruins of the temple of Phoebus

Apollo at Cumae. It was beneath this temple that Sibylla's famous shrine lay.

As might be imagined, the Oracle was mightily offended by this (she was, after all, beloved of Apollo and accustomed to more deferential treatment). Consequently, she decamped and made her way through the series of underground cave systems that underpin the Italian peninsula to the *Grotto delle Fate*, or the Grotto of the Fates, an extensive limestone cavern through which an underground river runs. The entrance to the Grotto was but an hour's journey on foot along the same road that led from Montemonaco to our farm.

Here Sibylla had lived in peace and tranquility for many centuries, visited now and then by the occasional pilgrim or supplicant. Her counsel might have been more sought after, but she had made it abundantly clear early on that she was to be consulted on serious matters only. She became quite cranky if the problem brought to her seemed in any way frivolous. Although immortal, she was old and ill tempered by disposition.

Of course, she did have her favorites. My great-grandmother she had treated as a kind of confidante and my grandmother after her. In fact, it was Sibylla who taught my grandmother to read and write and do sums, who advised her that literacy and numeracy were mechanisms by which a woman might first obtain and then retain power. (My nonna taught my mother these arts, and my mother, in turn, schooled me and my sister in them. My dear father and noisy, impetuous brothers remained blissfully unschooled, as did the majority of my fellow Montemonaci.)

However, our special relationship with the Oracle had

roots other than the friendship that existed between her and the women of my family. The road to the Grotto ran past our house. Therefore, it fell to us to act as gatekeepers to the Grotto and, understanding full well that we owed our prosperity in large measure to Sibylla's good graces, we took our responsibilities in this regard very seriously indeed. Which is why the sudden appearance of a small band of strangers coming 'round the bend in the bumpy road that led from San Sebastiano toward the grotto put my parents immediately on their guard.

It was coming onto Evensong, mid-May, warm enough by day, but still cool by night. My mother, Concetta, and I were in the midst of preparing a meal outside under a pergola constructed for that purpose a little distance from the house—the farmhouse had only slits for windows and cooking inside created a great deal of smoke. When the weather was clement, as it was much of the year, we cooked outside.

At the time, Mama would have been in her mid-thirties, a sturdy, blocky woman who wore her hair—dark and liberally streaked with gray even then—in a thick braid down her back. Concetta was sixteen—pretty, sweet-tempered, docile, and a little dull with ample curves and brown eyes like a doe. I was eighteen months her junior and more closely resembled a small boy than a woman—that is to say, I was slight and wiry and in no way possessed of anything that might be described as a figure.

"I'm putting you in charge of chopping," Mama told Concetta. "As for you, Mariuccia, it's your turn to sauté the vegetables until they are soft. Soft, not burnt! Golden, not brown!" She waved her big wooden spoon menacingly at me, for I was inclined to daydream and could not be counted on to concentrate to the degree required to cook vegetables properly without some vigilance on her part. Nor, in fact, was I much interested in the womanly arts. I was a bold girl, sturdy and strong, and more interested in hunting wolves alongside my father or tending the goats on the mountain than cooking up a skillet of wild greens or a pot of beans.

Just then a voice called out, "Hallo!" and glancing up, we spotted a small party of men round the bend in the dusty road that led from the village past our farm on its way to the Grotto.

Papa glanced up from the otter's pelt he was stretching on a frame, then raised his hand in greeting. "Hallo!"

My mother left the cook fire to join him, and Concetta and I stepped out from under the pergola, wiping our hands on our aprons and craning our necks to have a better view. These were strangers—we could see that straightaway—and, as there were not often strangers in those parts, their arrival was a matter of some interest.

At the head of the party shuffled a roughly clad boy in wooden clogs. He looked to be about Concetta's age and was half leading, half dragging a reluctant donkey, on the back of which wobbled an old priest who looked, even from that distance, as brittle as glass. A stooped, heavy-set man wearing a sweat-stained linen shirt, broadcloth breeches, and dusty jackboots strode alongside the donkey, his hand on its neck as if to steady the creature. Bringing up the rear was a portly young man in his late twenties, wielding a stout walking stick and attired in what I now know to be smart Alpine gear, although at the time nothing could have seemed so out of place and preposterous as his black lederhosen, trimmed with light-green embroidery and held up by black suspenders, a white shirt with a silver-ringed red tie, and a hat of dark-green felt with a feather poking out of its band. His choice of costume was rendered particularly unfortunate by the fact that he sported a significant belly, which strained at the buttons that held his shirt together, while his legs, by way of contrast, were skinny, hairy, and slightly bowed. On catching sight of us, he signaled to his party to remain where they were and swaggered toward us—large and doughy with brown, swimming eyes and full red lips—I have observed that it is impossible for someone wearing lederhosen to walk normally.

"Hallo there! Salutations!" this fine fellow greeted my father. "Are you, by chance, Signor Umbellino?"

"The same!" My father—grizzled, humorous, and lacking in teeth—wiped his hands on his flanks. "And, you, Signor, who might you be?"

"I am Signor Cesare Bacigalupo from the town of Casteldurante in the diocese of Urbino and I have the distinction of being Prior of that city's Confraternity of Good Death and...*hmmph*...I also happen to own Bacigalupo & Son, Producers and Exporters of fine majolica ware." He ducked his head, twirled his black mustachios, and added, "It has been in my family for several generations. Perhaps you've heard of it?"

"I have not," my father admitted genially. "However, as

I have discovered in the course of all my many years on the dear Lord's earth, there is much I have not heard of and I have never ventured farther north than the town of Ascoli Piceno. But have your men advance. We Umbellini are not brigands. Nor do we bite unless the occasion requires, in which case we most assuredly do."

Cesare turned and waved to the party of travelers to approach.

The boy yanked at the donkey's halter. The donkey, in turn, balked, at which point the stooped fellow cried, "Yee ha!" and slapped the beast on the rear. This had the effect of startling the donkey into activity, as a consequence of which four of them—the donkey, the priest riding the donkey, the boy leading the donkey, and the man traveling alongside the donkey—catapulted forward. They came to a jolting halt about five feet away from our family.

"And who might you be, Venerable Monsignor?" my father asked the priest.

"Only poor old Padre Eusebio from Capella Cola in Casteldurante," the priest informed him gloomily. "And, I must tell you straightaway, good man, I am here under protest."

"Are you being kidnapped?" my father asked.

"Pay him no mind," said the heavy-set man. "He is never happy, no matter the circumstances. As for me, I am Pio Assaroti, lay sacristan to Padre Eusebio here and a fellow member of the Confraternity of Good Death, and this is my son Pasquale." He indicated the boy leading the donkey.

"A pleasure and an honor, Signori!" My father bowed to the party. "And this is my wife Esperanza and my many children. But, tell me: What business brings you to these parts?"

"Monkey business!" Father Eusebio spat out. "Sheer madness!"

"Now, Padre," Cesare chided him, then, turning to my father, "We come on very important business, indeed! The *Pope's* business, to be precise."

"You don't say!" My father was impressed. "The Pope himself! And what business would His Holiness have in our remote parts?"

"Why, the business of Our Lord, of course!" Cesare replied. And you can help by pointing us in the direction of a place called the Grotto delle Fate."

At this, we Umbellini gave a collective gasp and looked at one another in surprise and dismay. It was well understood on Monte Vettore that neither the Grotto nor its inhabitant was to be discussed in the presence of clergy or anyone connected with the church. Nothing connected with the old religion was.

"Pardon me," my father said warily, "but of what possible interest to His Holiness is an old cave in a faraway place?"

"Do not be shocked, but His Holiness has heard that people visit this cave in order to consult a pagan sorceress," Cesare informed us. "Obviously this is of the gravest concern to the Holy Father. Black magic, you know." He shook his head. "Very bad!"

"Yes, well, perhaps," my father said. "But what you describe has been going on for a very long time. What does the Pope propose to do about it?"

"His Holiness has charged us with sealing off the entrance

to the cave with explosives," Cesare explained. "We are going to use black gunpowder, a mixture of saltpeter, sulfur, and charcoal. It's the latest thing. The Chinese invented it. It's remarkably effective."

My parents looked at one another, struggling to maintain their composure. "I don't know..." my father began.

"It's very risky," my mother agreed.

At this Padre Eusebio seemed to rally. Sitting up straight on the donkey he asked in a creaky voice, "You too, have reservations? What are your concerns, good people?"

"If you seal off the entrance to the cave, you will anger the Old One," my father replied. "I think you will agree, Father, that angering an Old One is never a good idea."

My mother pointed to a scrap of wolf fur and bells dangling from a piece of red yarn tied around the donkey's neck. "That may ward off the Evil Eye, Padre, but it won't protect you from the Old One's wrath."

"You see!" Padre Eusebio turned accusingly to Cesare. "I knew this was a terrible idea. Pio! Pasquale! Get me down off this infernal donkey! I'm not going a step farther!"

"Don't be ridiculous! What could possibly happen?" Cesare protested.

Seeing the sacristan and Pasquale start to half wrestle, half drag the priest from the donkey's back, I rushed forward and grabbed hold of the pack animal's reins to steady it during the untidy procedure.

"Mari!" my mother cautioned. "Let Carmine do that!"

Carmine stepped forward and I reluctantly handed the reins to him.

"What might come of angering the Old One?" my father

asked. "Why, storms so fierce that crops are destroyed over a large region."

"Floods," suggested my mother. "Of course, these would only affect towns in the valleys—your own town of Casteldurante, for example. Then there are earthquakes."

"Let's not forget rock slides."

"And mudslides! Whole villages have been known to—"

Padre Eusebio, who, by now, had both feet on the ground, shook a warning finger at Cesare and declared, "You see, Prior! I told you this was a fool's errand, but, no! You forced me to ride two full days in a wretched stagecoach over appalling roads, before dragging me halfway up this accursed mountain, on a donkey so bony, up a goat path so rutted that I feel as if I've been bumped in a sack over rocks for the past five hours!"

My mother shot a quick glance at my father—she looked worried. He nodded curtly to signal that he understood her concern, then cleared his throat. "If I may presume to offer you gentlemen a little advice?"

"But, of course!" replied Cesare.

"Abandon this enterprise. Trust me when I tell you that it cannot end well."

"Out of the question," Cesare replied. "It is His Holiness who has asked this of us and you can't say 'no' to His Holiness."

Papa sighed. "Then it is one Old One against another. In any case, I would encourage you to stop here for the night and continue on your journey tomorrow. It is an hour yet to the Grotto, the light is fading, and the way is treacherous enough when the sun is high in the sky."

"To get to the grotto, you must pass through the *Gola*

dell'Infernaccia itself—the Throat of Hell!" Mama shook her head. "Not a thing I would undertake in the dark."

Padre Eusebio turned to Pio. "The Throat of *Hell?*"

"Not only would you have difficulty finding your way there in the dark, you would not wish to remain there after sunset, especially on a Monday," my mother said. "I'm referring, of course, to the Lamiae."

"What in Heaven's name are Lamiae?" Cesare demanded. He sounded exasperated.

"Shapeshifters who attend on Sibylla," my mother replied. "Ordinarily they look like beautiful women, quite small, but every Saturday night, they turn into snakes and go writhing about the mountain meadows. They are highly poisonous. No one who has been bitten by a Lamia has lived to tell the tale."

"When do they turn back into beautiful women?" Pasquale wanted to know.

"Not until Monday, when the Pope says Mass," Papa said. "Now today's Monday, but has the Pope said Mass?" He shrugged. "Who knows? Perhaps he is ill. Perhaps he is en route somewhere. Perhaps he is relaxing at one of his country estates. So, you see, gentlemen, there's no way of telling what you might encounter up there on the crag. Ours is the last farm beyond Montemonaco. Take supper with us and a night's rest and continue on your way in the morning."

"We accept your generous invitation," Padre Eusebio said, glancing daggers at Cesare. "Now, where can I sit down? I feel all at sixes and sevens! If the Pope cares so much about this witch, why doesn't he come and deal with her himself? He's a younger man than me, yes, by a dozen years. Besides,

leave well enough alone! Let sleeping witches lie!" Seizing
Rinardo by one elbow and Emilio by the other with hands
that did not so much shake as vibrate, he cried querulously,
"Lads, take me to a chair!"

Cesare looked at Pio and shrugged. "May as well humor
him. Only a priest can perform the banishing ritual; we need
him for that." He turned back to my parents and bowed with a
flourish. "It would seem that we are accepting your kind invitation to stay the night. And now, Signor Umbellino, perhaps
you might do me the honor of introducing your beautiful
daughters to me." His gaze, rheumy and red-rimmed, fixed
on pretty Concetta. "Unless they are not daughters at all, but
Lamiae!"

Concetta blushed and cast her eyes down. Then she
looked up to meet his gaze. To my surprise, she looked
pleased, even very pleased.

"This is my eldest daughter, Concetta," my father told
him. "And this tadpole of a girl here…" He ruffled my unruly
hair. "This is Mariuccia."

"Pleased to make your acquaintance," the Prior said,
bowing, it must be noted, more in the direction of my sister
than myself.

"Pleased to make yours," said Concetta and blushed
again.

"Take care of the donkey, while I see to Padre," Pio told
Pasquale and headed over to where my brothers had deposited the old priest in a chair under a big oak tree close to the
house.

"Is there somewhere I can stable the donkey?" Pasquale
asked Papa.

"Mari will show you," replied my father.

"This way," I said to Pasquale and started toward the stable.

The boy followed. "Are there really such creatures as Lamiae?"

"Of course."

"Have you ever seen one?"

"Never. If I had, I would not be alive today." Here I became inventive. "You can hear them, though. The Lamiae. At night. They make a most peculiar noise—very shrill." In fact, peacocks were plentiful on our mountain and could frequently be heard—day or night—uttering their distinctive shrill cry. "If you hear such a sound," I warned him solemnly, "you must be very sure not to go outside, not for anything. Not if you wish to live to see another day."

"Who would have known that the countryside was full of such terrors?" Pasquale wondered. He crossed himself.

The evening that followed lives on in my memory as a disjointed series of overheard conversations, intrigue, and stolen moments. It began with a pitched, if surreptitious battle between Concetta and myself up in the loft that served as our bedroom and concerned her hairbrush—a terrific bone of contention between us. Papa had made it for her from the bristles of a wild boar; he had fashioned a similar one for Mama when they were first married and had promised me my own brush when next he felled a boar. However, boars, as it turned out, were few and far between that year; fully six months had passed since his crossbow had taken down the one from whose bristles he had crafted Concetta's brush. In the meantime, I was supposed to make do with a comb carved from the bone of a deer. In my opinion this was incredibly unfair.

"What am I supposed to do?" I demanded. "You know how thick my hair is? Do you want me to look like a walking bramble bush?"

"Why should I care what you look like? It is me that has to look good, not you!"

"Who for? That fat Prior?"

"He is not fat!"

"With that big belly and those spindly legs? He looks like a puffed-up pigeon!"

"You're just jealous because he likes me, not you. It's my brush and I don't want your greasy hairs all through it!" I've said that Concetta was sweet, but she had her moments—all big sisters do—and this was one of them.

"But I've got *mats!*" I protested.

"You've also got lice and burrs—more reason for me not to let you use it!"

"I do not!"

"Do so!"

"Concetta!" my mother trilled from downstairs. This was her fake voice, put on for show. "I need your help preparing a bed for our guests!"

The Prior's evident interest in my sister had not been lost on my parents. How could it have been? He had been making eyes at Concetta from the moment of their introduction—big, wet dog eyes. Sickening, I thought, but she evidently liked it. I suppose that the fact that he came from faraway and clearly possessed both means and social standing made him that much more attractive to her. I am told that these things matter to girls, though they have never mattered much to me.

Just before we had climbed up the ladder to the loft to tidy ourselves up and put on fresh aprons over our red skirts, I had overhead a whispered exchange between my mother and my father. "What a good match!" my mother said. "You don't suppose he's married, do you?"

"I'm one step ahead of you," replied my father. "I asked him…in a very offhanded way, of course…whether he was the Bacigalupo or the Son in Bacigalupo & Son. And he replied, 'I was the son until my father died and now I am the Bacigalupo. There is, at the present moment, no son, there being, as yet, no wife.'"

To which my mother had replied, "Perfect! A Prior and a prosperous business owner! Too bad that he lives so far away. Still, it can't be helped. Listen to me, Umberto, we must make certain to put her in his path as often as possible."

In retrospect, I don't blame my parents for their conspiring in the matter of my sister and Cesare Bacigalupo. They had two marriageable daughters and Montemonaco was a small mountain village—remote and isolated. If there is one thing people who keep livestock know, it's the danger of too much inbreeding and there was no boy our age in the village who was not some kind of cousin to us. Still, the fact that they would so blithely entertain the notion of sending my sister to live so far away from us and with such a ridiculous man struck me at the time as somehow traitorous.

Concetta gave her long lustrous hair a couple of concerted brushes and tied a white embroidered scarf around her shoulders before thrusting the disputed hairbrush under her pillow. She adjusted her corselet, tightening the red laces so that her figure might be shown to its best advantage, then, "Coming!" she cried—sounding all sweetness. To me she hissed, "I mean it, Mari! Don't you dare use my brush!" And she climbed hand over hand down the ladder from our loft.

I responded by sticking my tongue out at her. "Or you'll do what to me?" Retrieving her brush from under her pillow, I proceeded to brush my coarse mop of hair vigorously before returning the brush to its hiding place. There were a few burrs in it, I must admit—this evidence of my crime I removed from the bristles, dropping them out the casement window onto the yard below—but there were most emphatically no lice and never had been. So there, I thought, and, righting my skirt, straightening my apron, and tying my own scarf around my shoulders with a sigh—for I always felt ridiculous in that getup—I followed my pretty sister down the ladder to where Mama was standing beside the clothes press, a towering heap of bedding in her arms.

No sooner had she divided the heap between the three of us, however, than Carmine ran into the house and announced, "Papa says to stop what you're doing and come outside. Padre Eusebio has something *amazing* to show us!"

We rushed outside with our armful of bedding to find our guests seated in chairs dragged by my brothers from the house to a spot underneath the big oak tree. My father had provided the Castelduranteans with small earthenware cups filled with mistà and I could see at a glance that the brew had begun to have the desired effect; Pio, Pasquale, the Prior, and my father seemed relaxed, cheerful, and expansive. Only Padre Eusebio, slumped in his chair with his arms folded tightly across his chest and a scowl on his face, appeared petulant and aggrieved.

"What is it?" my brothers clamored. "What does Padre have to show us? We want to see it! Show it to us!"

Cesare cleared his throat. "It is something truly wondrous. His Holiness himself lent it to Padre for the duration of this mission. A relic of St. Alphonsus De Ligouri. It will serve to protect him should the need arise."

"*Pffit!*" Padre Eusebio made a disdainful gesture involving his hand and his chin. "St. Alphonsus is the patron saint of arthritis. I very much doubt his powers extend to warding off witches."

"Still...a relic!" My father was impressed. "You have to admit it: A relic is something you don't see every day!"

I leaned over and whispered to Mama, "What's a relic?"

"A piece of a dead saint's body," she whispered back.

"*Ew!*"

"Go on, Padre," Pio urged the priest. "Show everyone the relic."

"Oh, all right! If I must!" The priest removed a small, elaborately carved ivory box from inside his cassock and, opening it, held it out for us to see. Inside was something resembling a cigar butt.

"What is it?" Carmine asked.

"Why, it's the blessed saint's big toe!" Cesare replied. "His left one."

Eusebio snapped the lid of the box shut and replaced it

inside his cassock. "Do you know what I think? I think His Holiness gave me this toe as a prank. That scoundrel bishop, the one who sent us on this accursed mission, he must have told him about me. You know the one I'm talking about. Adeodatus the High and Mighty. That man has never liked me."

"Come, girls, we must prepare beds for our guests," my mother reminded us. Concetta and I started to turn away, which brought Cesare instantly to his feet.

"Do you mind if I accompany you?" Cesare asked Concetta. "I have a cramp I should like to walk out."

My parents exchanged a glance and Mama said, "Of course," whereupon the four of us headed off in the direction of the lean-to where we put up stray travelers, the occasional peddler, or revelers who had drunk too must mistà to make it safely home—it was spare, but dry and possessed of both a roof and a place out of the wind to make a fire.

And so it continued for the remainder of that evening. Cesare strutted and postured and pontificated and fawned, falling all over himself to impress Concetta, while my sister, for her part, demurred and blushed and allowed herself to be impressed—all this under the watchful and deeply interested gaze of my parents. By the time Papa, lantern in hand, escorted our visitors to the lean-to and Mama blew out the last candle, I had had it up to here with the whole Concetta and Cesare courting thing and was ready to see the last of the Castelduranteans and to return to life on the mountain as usual.

But, although I did not know it at the time, that was never again to be the case.

That night, after everyone else in the house had retired, Mama crept out of bed, climbed up the ladder to our loft, and gently shook me awake. "What...?" I began, but she laid a finger on my lips, shook her head and looked pointedly at Concetta who lay beside me, her dark hair spread out across the pillow, her chest expanding and contracting gently with her breath. Mama jerked her head to one side, indicating that I was to follow her.

Probably something to do with the goats, I reckoned. Maybe Diana, our newest little mother to be, was having her baby, although it was surely too early for that. When Mama needed help with her herd, I was the one she relied on. The boys were too rough and Concetta didn't care for goats—which I couldn't understand, there being few more dependable or, for that matter, more charming creatures than goats.

I rubbed my eyes, hastily threw a shawl around my shoulders and, still stupid with sleep, followed Mama down the ladder and out of the house. It was the time of the new Willow Moon and very dark. She fetched the bull's-eye lantern from its nail by the door, lit it, and, by the pale yellow light it cast, set out not for the goat barn, to my surprise, but in the direction of the olive grove. I ran after her and, catching hold of her sleeve, tugged on it. "I don't understand. Where are we going?"

"To warn Lady Sibylla."

If she had doused me with a bucket of icy water, it couldn't have woken me up faster. Visiting the Oracle was something women did, not girls, and I had just turned fifteen. "But what about Concetta?" I asked.

"Concetta is too timid. You do not frighten so easily. Now come along and hurry. We have only until the dawn to do what we must do."

Beyond the stone mill where Papa ground his olives to paste before pressing them for oil, was the steep and twisting goat path that led from our farm to the grotto. It was a secret shortcut, known only to Montemonaci—by taking the path instead of the main road, a supplicant could bypass the Gola dell'Infernaccia entirely and arrive at the grotto in half the time.

Accordingly, some thirty minutes after we set forth, we arrived at the grotto's shield-shaped entrance high up on the mountain. Dropping to her knees and holding the lantern out before her, Mama crawled through the opening (it was only three feet high) and into the Oracle's antechamber. This was a low-ceilinged and damp smelling place, perhaps ten feet long and six wide, unremarkable save for a pair of ornate bronze doors that glinted at its far end. On either side of the antechamber a rough bench had been hewn out of the rock. Mama placed the lantern on the bench and we sat down gingerly. "We will wait here," she told me.

"Will she come out? Or do we go in?" I asked.

"Neither. When Milady consents to an interview, those doors there creak slowly open and you hear a voice coming from someplace deep inside the mountain. It doesn't sound quite human. More like the wind would if the wind had a voice."

"Just her voice?" I was disappointed.

Mama nodded. "No one has actually seen the Lady Sibylla for…I don't know how long. From before my grand-mother was born. I have twice called upon her, once to assist me in minimizing the ill effects of a particularly stubborn case of *mal'occhia* that had affected my entire herd of goats—that was before you were born—and once in an effort to save the life of a dear child who had fallen ill with typhus. You remember little Giuseppe?"

I nodded. Giuseppe was buried in the cemetery of our small church, alongside little Rosaria, the baby who had lived for not even a week.

"One does not come to the Oracle for every little thing," Mama told me. "You have to be selective, to pick and choose. 'I am not a wishing well!' she told me once, and I have tried to respect that. Tonight, however…tonight is an altogether different matter. Tonight, we come to warn her of the danger to come."

Twenty long minutes passed and I was beginning to wish that Mama had chosen Concetta rather than me or, at the very least, that I had taken something warmer than my red shawl—it was cold and the bench very hard—when we heard a slipping, sliding noise near the cave's entrance and saw by the lantern's golden light an emerald green serpent gliding rapidly toward us—a Lamia, the first I had ever seen.

Mama greeted the snake. "Good evening to you."

"Good evening to you," the snake hissed in reply.

"I see that the Pope has yet to say Mass."

"Apparently. He's a bit of a slacker, that one. But what brings you to Milady's antechamber at this time of night,

Esperanza Umbellino? And who is this child? You know how Milady feels about children. She finds them tedious in the extreme."

"Bad news, I'm afraid," Mama replied. "And this is my daughter Mariuccia. She looks younger than her years, but she is fifteen, scarcely a child, and I hope she shall prove a help to me and Milady in this dark hour."

"Bad news? Dark hour? What are you talking about? You're frightening me!"

"Holy Father has sent a foolish old priest and a pompous prior to seal up this cave. They think Sibylla is a witch. We did our best to frighten them out of it, but I think they will do it all the same. Tomorrow morning, most likely."

"Catastrophe!" shrilled the Lamia, and, in her dismay, she began to wriggle frenetically about. Lamiae, as a species, are easily excited, fearful by nature, and much given to hysteria and hyperventilation. This one was no exception. "Disaster! Utter, utter calamity!"

"Calm yourself, please!" Mama implored the serpent. "Now is not the time to lose our wits. We haven't much time if we are to save Sibylla. Now, listen up. I thought, perhaps, we could take her home with us—"

"Oh!" replied the snake and stopped wriggling. "Oh, Esperanza and Mariuccia Umbellino, I don't know if such a plan would work. You see, Sibylla, well, she's very…how shall I put this? She's *shy!*"

"Given the direness of the situation, shyness is a luxury she can ill afford."

"You don't understand." It was evident that the Lamia was attempting to choose her words with the utmost care.

"Sibylla hasn't been…well, *seen* by anyone for I don't know how long! Do you take my meaning?"

"I don't!" I could tell Mama was becoming increasingly exasperated with the empty-headed, mincing serpent. "What? Is she concerned she doesn't look her best? She's more than a thousand years old!"

"I think it's fair to say that Milady Sibylla…"

At this the bronze doors creaked suddenly open and the Sibyl demanded, "Snake! Are you telling tales out of school?"

The serpent reared up, emitted her shrill peacock cry, then undulated rapidly out the entrance of the grotto and into the night.

"And don't you come back until the Pope says Mass, you useless creature!" Sibylla called after her, then paused. "Who is in my antechamber? I smell human beings!"

"It's Esperanza Umbellino, Milady," Mama said hurriedly, "and my daughter Mariuccia Umbellino."

"What's wrong with her?"

"Nothing, thanks be. She's well."

"So, what is it then that brings you here in the dead of night, dragging your daughter along with you like a cat does a kitten?" demanded the Oracle. "Why have you woken me from my sleep if not for a sickly child or some curse or other?"

"Something that concerns you directly, Milady," my mother said. "The Pope has sent a party of men to seal off your grotto with black gunpowder."

"Black gunpowder? What is this black gunpowder? I've never heard of it."

"I haven't the slightest idea," Mama replied. "But it's supposed to be very effective."

There was a silence, then, "Bother! What a bore! How am I supposed to find another cave? As if twice in a millennium weren't enough! These awful churchmen! They'll stop at absolutely nothing! No live and let live for them and no respect whatsoever for their elders! They're simply impossible, that's what!"

"I thought we could take you with us," Mama suggested. "Now. Tonight. We could hide you away, then, once the Castelduranteans are gone, the men of Montemonaco could dig out the cave and you could come home."

"No, no." Sibylla sounded very distracted. "Won't work."

"Why not?"

"Out of the question."

"Why?"

"I wouldn't dream of it!"

Mama sighed. "But, Milady, it would be such an honor—"

The Oracle interrupted her. "Yes, yes. I'm sure it would, but it's quite impossible. You see, I am not...as I once was."

"Who of us is? Believe it or not, I was once quite the beauty! These things pass."

"It's not just my looks," Sibylla told us. "How can I explain this so that you will understand?" She paused. Then, "I have shrunk."

"That's only natural," Mama pointed out. "I am shorter than I was as a maid and my nonna—"

"No, you don't understand," Sibylla stopped her. "When I say *shrunk*, I mean, really shrunk. Really, really shrunk."

Mama considered this information for a moment. "So how small are you?"

"So small that I no longer have an actual body." Sibylla sounded bitter and wistful at the same time. "All that remains of me is my voice."

We were stunned by this revelation. "How can that be? How could such a thing happen?" Mama asked.

"It's a long story and one I'm not up to telling at the moment. Too depressing."

"So, if you are only a voice," I blurted out, "how do you get from place to place?"

"Mariuccia!" Mama scolded.

"It's a reasonable question," the Sibyl replied. "The answer is I don't. I just…stay in my jug."

"Your jug?"

"It's very disconcerting to be disembodied," Sibylla explained. "One always feels as though parts of one might break away and drift off. Because, after all, that did happen. It's how I lost the rest of me. So I stay in my jug. It makes me feel safer…more contained. It's a very nice jug!"

"So, why don't we just take your jug home with us then?" Mama urged her. "No one needs to know what's inside."

"I suppose that might be…possible," Sibylla entertained the idea.

"I have a goatskin pouch with me. I could carry your jug in that."

"That might be all right," reflected Sibylla.

"We swear to you that we will tell no one of your…condition and that we will return you to your home as quickly as possible. Don't we, Mariuccia?"

I nodded vigorously. "Oh, yes."

"Well, all right then," Sibylla agreed. "But first you must come down and fetch me."

Icy fear washed over me. No mortal person had ever entered the Oracle's inner sanctum; at least, that is what we had always been told. "Enter your…shrine?" Mama asked the Oracle. "Are you sure?"

"I would have one of those silly Lamiae bring me to you, but, at present, they are sadly lacking in the hand department," Sibylla informed us. "If the Pope would only get around to saying Mass instead of spending all of his time creating trouble for beings like myself, we wouldn't be in this fix!"

"We won't…turn to stone or anything?" Mama asked carefully.

"Of course not! What do you think I am? A gorgon? Just watch your step! The descent is slippery. It's a cave."

At this, the doors yawned slightly more open, as if the mountain was exhaling. From within pulsed a kind of greenish glow, the same metallic color a firefly emits.

Mama took a deep breath and, seizing hold of my arm with one hand and holding the lantern aloft with the other, she led me through the doors into a vast chamber spottily lit by patches of phosphorescence. A forest of sand-colored columns—stalagmites—twirled up from the floor of the grotto and stalactites like huge icicles of dripping rock reached down from a ceiling so high above us that we could not make it out. We seemed to be standing on a kind of rough staircase hewn from limestone, but only just—more like a ramp sloping toward what I could only assume was the bottom of at least this one chamber of the grotto. This was as much as we could discern; the cave was thick with rock formations; we did not have a clear view.

"Don't just stand there gawping!" Sibylla complained. "Come get me!" The Oracle's voice, much amplified, seemed to come from everywhere and from nowhere at the same time.

Mama appeared disoriented. "But where exactly are you?"

"Down here by the disappearing spring," she replied.

Mama lifted the lantern, then lowered it, then lifted it again. "I think I might see your jug!" She pointed. "See, Mariuccia, down there!"

Something glinted all right, catching at the light.

"I see it!" I cried. "And I hear water!"

"Be careful!" Mama warned me as we edged our way sideways down the ramp—it was steeply pitched and very slippery. "*Addio!* The last thing we need is for one of us to break a leg!"

Finally reaching the bottom of the ramp, we picked our way through a grove of needle-sharp stalagmites to a little silver wriggle of a stream that writhed snakelike along the floor of the cave before disappearing into the rock. And there it was: a squat amber jug with a trefoil mouth shaped like a clover leaf and a thick turquoise handle.

"Well?" asked Sibylla proudly. "How do you like my jug? It's from Aleppo in Syria. Very fine workmanship. Someone brought it to me once. Can't remember who."

"It's very handsome," Mama replied.

I remember thinking how very odd it was to talk to a jug. Then I reminded myself that Mama wasn't talking to a jug, but to a voice *in* a jug—which was also pretty strange.

"You must be careful with my jug," Sibylla cautioned. "It's very old."

"We will be very careful, indeed!" Mama assured her. "Mariuccia, give me your shawl." I did so reluctantly, for here in the bowels of the earth it was even colder than it had been in the chilly antechamber. Mama wrapped it around the jug and carefully placed the bundle in her goatskin pouch. "Ready to go?"

"As ready as I'll ever be!" Sibylla answered. "To tell you the truth, I'm rather excited. It's been such a long time since I've been out and about."

I realized it was rude to ask, but I couldn't help myself. "How can you see if you're only a voice?"

"Mariuccia!" Mama sounded scandalized.

"It's all right," replied Sibylla. "That too, is a fair question. How can I exist at all? What larynx produces the sounds I make; what lips shape them? What organ advises me what to say? I am a mystery, child, even to myself."

And with that we made our way back up the ramp, into the antechamber, and out into the cool May night. The skies were full of stars and I could just make out the Adriatic Sea glinting darkly to the east. As we started down the goat path toward the farm, we could hear a shrill sound from the meadow like peacocks crying.

"Those Lamiae!" the Sibyl complained affectionately. "Always a party for those girls! And why not? When I think of the body I used to have…"

"You and me both!" Mama replied.

"Are you walking funny?" asked Sibylla. "When did you start limping?"

"My buttocks are asleep. Next time around, let's do something about that awful stone bench. I'll have Umberto bring up some hay."

"Hay! What a good idea! Only, won't it get moldy?"

She sounded as happy, I thought, as a little bird in a warm spring rain.

The men from Casteldurante rose with the dawn.

Mama, upon our return from the grotto, had cleared a place in an old oak cabinet in the main room of the house for Sibylla's jug. Then she made everyone a big breakfast of black coffee, flatbread, figs, and *formaggio di fossa*, a strong-flavored goat's cheese that she aged in a limestone cave not far from the house. Having slept but a few hours, I kept nearly nodding off, causing Concetta to swat at me and complain, "What's wrong with you? I hope you don't expect me to serve everyone by myself!" I was awake enough, however, to note that Prior Bacigalupo looked just as ridiculous in the morning light as he had at twilight—and told her so.

While Mama, Concetta, and I cleaned up, Papa rubbed his full belly and pointed to the sun, still wobbling on the horizon as yellow as an egg yolk. "Best be on your way if you want to arrive before midday. My sons, assist these gentlemen in their packing!"

While Carmine, Emilio, and Rinardo were scrambling about the donkey with various bundles and parcels, Padre Eusebio emerged stiffly from the house, scratching his behind through his cassock with one hand and his nearly bald head with the other. He tottered, wincing, over to a chair set out in the yard and, easing himself down into it, declared, "I'm not feeling very well. Perhaps I'll just stay here and pray for your safe return."

"Nonsense!" said Prior Bacigalupo.

"But I am unwell!"

"You're going."

"But, Prior, it's Tuesday! *Tuesday!*" the old man pleaded.

"And what in Heaven's name is wrong with Tuesday?" Bacigalupo demanded.

"Every terrible thing that has ever happened to me personally happened on a Tuesday. It is my unlucky day."

"It's not just you, Padre," Mama said. "Tuesday is everyone's unlucky day. As my old nonna used to say, '*De Venere e di Marte né si sposa né si parte.*' Very unlucky to marry or embark upon a journey on a Tuesday…or a Friday, for that matter. That's because Tuesday is named after Mars, the Roman god of war, and Friday is named after Venus, the goddess of love. Mars and Venus. Those two cause a lot of trouble!"

"See!" Padre Eusebio crowed. "Tuesdays are very bad luck. I'm not just making it up!"

"That's ridiculous!" the Prior blustered. "We live in an age of reason…of science! There's nothing wrong with Tuesdays! Tuesdays are a perfectly good sort of day."

"They are a terrible, fearful sort of day," the priest insisted. "Awful things always happen on a Tuesday!"

The Prior took a deep breath and made an effort to compose himself. "See here, Father, there's absolutely no point in going on without you. You know that! Pio and I can't perform the banishing ritual. Only a priest can do that and we are both laymen."

"Did we not pass a church not a mile down the road?" Eusebio asked. "Why not ask the priest of that church to do the banishing ritual? Maybe he doesn't have a hammer-toe. Maybe he doesn't have bunions. Maybe Tuesday is *his* lucky day!"

Prior Bacigalupo sighed and turned to Papa. "Signor Umbellino, do you think we might impose upon your pastor to assist us?"

Papa looked dubious. "I very much doubt it. Our Padre DiNardo is blind. He never learned to read and he can't speak Latin. He wouldn't know what words to say."

"He can't read?" the Prior exclaimed. "How can he say Mass?"

"He acts it out," said Papa.

"It's very entertaining," Mama added. "The children love it."

The Prior turned back to Padre Eusebio. "You see? You're the only one who can do it. Do you really want me to tell Bishop Adeodatus that you refused a direct order from Rome? You know how unpleasant he can be! And he doesn't like you much to begin with."

Eusebio cringed. "That is true. Oh, all right! Help me up on this terrible creature then. Let's get this dreadful muddle over with. Mark my words, though. Embarking on a Tuesday…insulting a sorceress…. Misfortune will surely come of this foolhardy endeavor!"

Pio and Pasquale hoisted the priest off the ground and

onto the back of the donkey. The sacristan applied a willow switch to the donkey's hindquarters. She tottered forward, then balked and registered her objection by rolling her eyes and braying.

"See!" Eusebio pointed out. "Not even the infernal donkey wants to go!"

"*Avanti!*" cried the Prior and, brandishing his walking stick as though it were a baton, he took his place at the head of the party.

"Good-bye! Good-bye!" we cried, waving, as the Castelduranteans headed up the road toward the Gola dell'Infernaccia.

"We hope you will join us for lunch on your return!" Mama shouted after them.

"Watch out for wolves and vipers!" Papa cried.

"Mind the witches and demons!" we children chorused.

When they had disappeared from sight, I tugged at Mama's sleeve. "Why are we asking them to lunch when they're about to blow up the sacred grotto?"

"The same reason we invited them to dinner last night," Mama replied. "We are being hospitable. Besides, as a wise man once said, keep your friends close and your enemies closer."

In the meantime, Papa had turned to the boys and was rubbing his hands together in excitement. "Who wants to go see if this new black gunpowder really works?"

"We do!" they cried. "Hooray!"

"What about me?" I was exhausted from being up half the night, but I did not want to miss so grand a thing as an explosion.

Papa shook his head. "No, no, Mariuccia, you must remember that you are a girl and, besides, you have to help Mama make lunch."

"Concetta can help Mama," I pleaded. "She's a better cook than me. I burn everything."

"She's right about that," said Mama. "Let her go with you, Umberto. Concetta and I can manage."

"But, Mama!" Concetta began.

"Don't you start," Mama told her. "An explosion would only frighten you and, besides, how am I going to make lunch for so many with only two hands?"

Papa pinched my sister's plump cheek and, inclining close to her, murmured, "You must look your very prettiest, *mia cara bambina*, for it has come to your mother's and my attention that Prior Cesare has taken quite a shining to you, and he is a rich and important gentleman."

At this Concetta blushed furiously and turned aside, casting her eyes down in pleasant confusion.

"Get out of here!" my mother instructed the rest of us. "Go on! You heard me! Shoo! I have work to do and I don't want you underfoot!"

Papa and the boys took off for the olive grove. I was just starting after them when I heard Mama tell Concetta, "I hope those fools don't do serious damage to the grotto! What will we do then? Thank goodness Sibylla is safe!" That stopped me in my tracks. Surely she wasn't telling Concetta *our* secret?

"What do you mean?" Concetta asked. "How can she possibly be safe? She's about to be entombed in a mountain!"

There was a moment of silence, then, "I have a little surprise for you."

Anger flooded me. Mama had chosen me, the brave daughter, to accompany her to the grotto; she had entrusted the secret of Sibylla's rescue to me, and now she was going to tell *Concetta?* I turned back toward the house and found the two of them standing before the old oak cabinet, the door of which was opened wide exposing jars filled with dried herbs, my mother's treasured Book of Shadows—a collection of spells and rituals that had belonged to her mother's great-grandmother—and the Oracle's antique jug.

"Lady Sibylla," Mama began in a respectful tone. "I would like to introduce you to my eldest daughter, Concetta."

Furious, I stamped my foot. Then, remembering that the most exciting thing ever to occur in the history of my little village was about to take place—and shortly—I turned and ran after my father and brothers up the goat path.

Because we had taken the shortcut to the grotto, we arrived a good twenty minutes before the party from Casteldurante straggled in, looking hot and very irritable. Papa had located a hiding place for us in a heaped tangle of rocks and scrub on the eastern ridge of the Gola dell'Infernaccia—the Throat of Hell. This was a narrow, twisting passage littered with the remains of eagle nests and the discarded bones of voles and mice and flanked by two walls of sheer rock for nearly a mile. It was, at the best of times, an arduous journey up the mountain from Montemonaco by way of the Gola—steep, sweltering, save in winter, and dusty always.

Upon their arrival in the clearing, the Prior spotted the distinctive shield-shaped entrance to the grotto and announced, "This must be the place!" Removing his Alpine hat, he mopped his brow with a big red handkerchief, while Padre Eusebio yanked at his Roman collar and made choking sounds.

"Get me off of this despicable devil-spawn!" he insisted; then, as Pio and Pasquale dragged him off the donkey, "Every bone in my body aches like a tooth!" The priest tottered to the edge of the clearing and plopped down on a rock. "*Ooch! Ooch!*" he complained. "My poor martyred feet—they are swollen to the size of cannon balls!" Removing a black lace fan from inside his cassock, he began to fan himself theatrically.

Pasquale, in the meantime, had ventured nearer to the grotto's entrance, and squatting down, peered inside. "Must be a pretty small witch."

"When it comes to witches," Padre Eusebio assured him, "size is of absolutely *no* consequence!"

The Prior took charge. "All right!" he announced, rubbing his big hands together. "The sooner we get this over with, the sooner we can head back. You, Pasquale and Pio, pour the gunpowder like so." Using the tip of his walking stick, he described a semicircle in the dirt in front of the grotto's entrance.

Pio extracted two horns of gunpowder from the donkey's saddlebags and handed one to Pasquale. "Remember: we don't want to use it all," he told his son. "Save some for the fuse. I'll start at this end, you at that. We'll meet in the middle."

When they had finished this task, Pio took Pasquale's

powder horn from him and combined its contents with those of his own horn. "Fetch the straw." While he trailed a thin line of powder away from the cave toward the perimeter of the clearing, Pasquale fetched a small bundle of straw from behind the saddle and, following along behind his father, strewed the hay alongside the trail of gunpowder. When this was done to Pio's satisfaction, he turned to the Prior. "Ready."

The Prior then turned to the priest. "Ready, Father."

Eusebio stopped fanning himself and stared incredulously at Bacigalupo. "Surely I pray *after* we've blown up the cave!"

"No," the Prior corrected him. "The Pope's instructions were for you to pray *before*."

"After!"

"Before!"

The priest glanced fearfully at the entrance to the grotto and hissed, "But what if the witch flies out on her broomstick and attacks me?"

"You've got St. Alphonsus's toe!"

"A lot of good that will do me! What am I supposed to do? Beat her off with it?"

Carmine and Emilio began to titter. Papa shushed them.

"I think Father Eusebio has a point," Pio interjected. "Better pray afterward, once we've bottled her up."

"Oh, all right!" the Prior conceded. "I suppose it doesn't make that much difference. Now, take cover, everyone, and remember to cover your mouths and noses with your handkerchiefs."

At this, Pio took the donkey's bridle and half-led, half-yanked her behind a cluster of large boulders, while Pasquale helped Padre Eusebio to his feet and steered him by one bony elbow to another group of boulders. All three removed handkerchiefs from their pockets and covered their mouths and noses with them while Papa, by a series of gestures culminating in his pulling his shirt over his head, indicated to my brothers that they should do the same. I covered my face with my apron.

As for the Prior, he removed a flint from the pocket of his lederhosen with a flourish and, turning in the direction of the grotto, addressed these words to its entrance, "As Prior of the Confraternity of the Good Death and emissary of His Holiness Pope Pius VII, I, Cesare Girolamo Bacigalupo, hereby send a message to Sibylla, so-called Queen of the Witches. Your reign here has ended!"

He knelt and, wiping the sweat from his brow with his big red handkerchief one last time, struck the flint. It took several tries for the flame to catch. When it did, Bacigalupo leapt to his feet, lingered for a moment to ensure that the modest fire would not flicker out halfway down the wick. Then he turned and scuttled for cover.

Carmine, Emilio, and Rinardo elbowed each other, smirking. "He runs like a girl!"

"*Respetto!*" Papa shook his head. "That is your future brother-in-law, if your mother gets her way."

"Huh?"

"*What?*"

"*Shhhh!*"

After what seemed like a rather long time, but was probably only two or three minutes, the flame licked and crackled its way up to the semicircle of gunpowder strewn before the cave's entrance. It caught and detonated with a boom so loud that for several minutes no one could hear anything at all. Rocks flew every which way. Boulders rumbled down the mountain, landing in front of the grotto's entrance and blocking it, and pebbles shot through the air like shrapnel. The explosion kicked up a yellow boil of acrid-smelling dust that took a few minutes to settle and made the eyes of all those in the vicinity smart and their nostrils burn and set off a chorus of sneezing and coughing. When it finally settled, everyone present could see that the blast had succeeded in its mission—the entrance to the grotto was no longer visible. It was completely blocked off by fallen rock. In fact, it looked as though the explosion had pulled down half the mountain.

In his hiding place, Papa shook his head. "Not good!"

"What do you mean, Papa?" Rinardo whispered. "It was *fantastic!*"

"You won't think it's so fantastic when we have to dig it out. *Che schiffo!* Black gunpowder! Who would have known? Our poor *padrona!* Has she even survived such an avalanche?" That was when I knew for sure that Mama had not told Papa of our escapade the night before; that he was unaware that Sibylla was safe in her jug back at our farm.

Down below in the clearing, Pasquale cried, "Ah, for sure she was a witch and we have blown up the gateway to Hell! If that's not the devil's stink filling my nose, I don't know what is!"

"That's the sulfur in the gunpowder," Pio pointed out.

"No putting it off any longer, Padre," the Prior Bacigalupo told the priest. "Pio, get Father's implements."

Opening the donkey's saddlebag, Pio extracted a large, oiled leather wallet and rooted through the ceremonial vestments, bone scrolls, rosaries, and prayer candles until he found a gilded vial of holy water, a small ivory salt box, and a white, fringed scarf or *stola*. He handed the vial and salt box to the priest and draped the stola around the old man's stooped shoulders.

Clearing his throat, Eusebio hobbled out into the clearing in front of the pile of rubble and began to pray at breakneck speed: "*Exorcizo te, omnis spiritus immeunde, in nomine Dei et in nomine Jesus Christi, Filii eius, Domini et Judicis nostri, et in virtute Spirtus Sancti…*"

Every few seconds, he glanced fearfully in the direction of the blocked entrance, as though he expected the Sibyl to burst through the rocks. As he mentioned each person of the Trinity, he made the sign of the cross, as did the rest of the party.

"Holy water!" Eusebio instructed Pio, who handed him the gilt vial. Eusebio unsealed it, tottered painfully over to the pile of rocks, flung its contents in the general direction of the sealed-up cave mouth, and then scurried back.

"Now the salt," he instructed Pio, who handed him the salt box. Opening it, Eusebio stood with his back to the cave's entrance and tossed a pinch of salt over his left shoulder. "Devil, be gone!" he instructed Satan and then glanced around at the rest of the party. "There! Satisfied? The witch is officially banished. If we leave now, we can make the Umbellino farm by lunchtime. And, just so you know, I'm planning to take a very long siesta this afternoon. I am too old for such goings on!"

We arrived back at the farm shortly after midday and about a half an hour in advance of the Castelduranteans. My brothers were hot and dusty, but exuberant and Papa only slightly less enthusiastic over the destruction we had witnessed. My own feelings were mixed. On the one hand, I lamented the ruin of what had for so many centuries been a holy place; on the other, I had just witnessed annihilation on a scale I had not hitherto known possible and, human nature being what it is, I found it hard not to be in some dark and unspeakable way thrilled by it.

"The explosion was terrific!" Papa told Mama and Concetta. "What a noise!" He clapped his hands. "Like that. Only much, much louder. And rocks everywhere. Flying through the air."

"You should have seen it, Mama!" Rinardo tugged at Mama's sleeve. "Such a *ka-boom* as you can't imagine! My ears are still ringing!"

"*Ka-boom! Ka-boom!*" Carmine and Emilio cried in unison and rushed about flailing their skinny arms in the air.

"All of you calm down!" Mama warned. "Remember, you're supposed to have been here all along. If you let on that you saw that explosion, I will cut off your ears and cook them in a stew! Mariuccia, change your apron. You look like you've been rolled downhill. You're covered with dust."

"And the fat Prior! You should have seen how he dived for cover!" Rinardo cried. Immediately Emilio and Carmine launched themselves through the air and, hitting the ground, rolled over and over again, giddy with excitement and choking with laughter.

"He is not fat!" Concetta cried, red-faced.

"He is so!"

"Get out of here if you can't be quiet!" Mama cried. "You are driving me crazy! Concetta, go and set the table for lunch."

Concetta stomped off indignantly in the direction of the olive grove, while the boys—who were like puppies really— clambered to their feet and ran, screeching and hooting and tumbling over one another, in the direction of the cowshed, leaving my parents and me alone in the yard.

"How badly damaged is the grotto?" Mama asked.

Papa shook his head and made a sucking sound with his teeth. "It is much worse than I could have imagined. This black gunpowder—truly it is the devil's own snuff!"

"Still, you can dig it out?"

"Of course! It will take time, that's all, and many hands. But I must tell you, Esperanza…" he took Mama's hand in both of his rough ones, "the Lady Sibylla…well, I can't see how she could have survived, immortal or not. The top of the mountain crashed into the grotto. The falling rock…surely it has crushed her."

Mama bit her lip and cast her eyes to one side, evidently considering the matter for a moment before yielding to sore temptation. My mother had many virtues; circumspection was not among them. "Can you keep a secret?" she began.

"Mama!" I objected. First Concetta, now Papa? Who next? The boys? If that were to be the case, we might as well shout the secret of Sibylla's salvation from the roof top!

Papa was honest to a fault. "That depends on how much mistà I have consumed," he replied.

"Come with me." Mama took him by the elbow and steered him into the house. I followed on their heels. She came to a halt before the old oak cabinet and opened its door. "What do you see before you?"

Papa squinted at the contents of the cabinet. "Herbs," he said. Then, "Your mother's Book of Shadows." He placed the palms of his hands on his haunches and leaned forward to have a closer look. He straightened up and pointed to the jug. "This jug here. I don't think I've ever seen that before!"

I groaned, but there was no stopping Mama now. She cleared her throat and addressed the jar. "Lady Sibylla, it gives me great honor to introduce you to my husband. Umberto, meet the Oracle of Cumae!"

After introductions were made, Mama removed the Book of Shadows from the shelf and handed it to me. "Take this to my room, Mariuccia," she instructed me. "And while you're at it, bring me your sister's hairbrush and leave it on my bed."

"Why me?" I objected. "It's her stupid hairbrush!"

"You heard me! Just do it!"

Disgruntled, I clambered up to our loft, seized Concetta's brush, and gave my own hair a vigorous brushing before descending the ladder and putting it with the Book of Shadows on my parents' bed. After all, my hair was probably full of yellow dust from the explosion and it wasn't as if I had my own brush.

The party from Casteldurante arrived at the farm half an hour later. The Prior, doubtless imagining himself a modern-day Crusader Knight, appeared enormously pleased with himself. He strode well in advance of his party, humming "Ave Maria" and brandishing his Alpine walking stick as though it were a pike, his chest thrust out like a pigeon and his chin held high. It was difficult not to notice how thick his waist was and how spindly his bare, hairy legs.

The remainder of his party, however, seemed distinctly fractious. Apparently Padre Eusebio had complained incessantly of headache since their departure from the grotto, while the sound of the explosion had so stupefied the donkey that she was quite beside herself. Pasquale and Pio had been compelled to take turns dragging her the entire way from the Gola to the farm. The balking of the donkey jolted the priest, which, in turn, made his headache worse, causing him to complain all the more vehemently.

"Help me off! Help me off!" Padre Eusebio bleated as soon as they reached the yard. He stretched his arms out like a child who wishes to be carried. Pasquale took one arm and Pio seized the other and, their patience with the old man exhausted, swung him off the donkey so unceremoniously that the priest landed on his troublesome feet with a jolt. He stood there for a moment, wobbling and clutching his forehead in his hands, until he had regained his balance. "I feel as though someone has driven an ice pick through my forehead!" he declared.

Mama took him by the arm. "Never mind, Padre! We have made you a beautiful lunch—a baked pasta such as you will never find in all the Marches—and, as for that poor head of yours, we shall stuff some mugwort up your nose. That will cure any headache."

"Really?" Padre Eusebio brightened. "Mugwort, you say?"

Mama turned to Concetta. "Fetch me some mugwort from the cabinet. Everyone else—there is a table laid for us in the olive grove."

As the Castelduranteans trooped off after Mama in the direction of the grove, Concetta whispered to me. "I can't open the cabinet…not with *her* in there! You do it!"

"Why me?"

"Because you're the brave one!"

"I may be brave, but I'm not stupid!"

Emilio, as it turned out, had been listening in. "Since when are you two afraid of a silly cabinet? I'll go get the mugwort."

"No!" I cried.

"Stop!" cried Concetta.

But Emilio was already racing for the house. I picked up my skirts and dashed after him, catching him by the arm halfway across the main room and yanking him backwards and off balance.

"What? What? You're hurting me!" Emilio protested. "What's going on?"

"Nothing! Just that it's important to get the right herb— the wrong one and you could kill the old priest. There's wolfbane in there and foxglove."

"I know what mugwort looks like the same as you!" Emilio wrenched his arm free.

"Who is that?" A voice, crackled with age, warbled out of the closed cabinet. "I hear a little boy!"

I panicked. "Sssshhh!"

"Who is that shushing me?" Sibylla sounded cross.

Releasing Emilio's arm, I sagged into a chair and pressed a hand to my forehead. "It's Mariuccia."

By this time Emilio's eyes had grown so wide that they were straining at their sockets. "Who are you talking to? Is it…*Nonna!*"

When my grandmother had died seven years before, Papa couldn't bring himself to accept that his beloved mother had passed. Everyone knows that in the period immediately following a death, the spirit of the departed is in a state of terrible shock—dazed, confused, and quite literally beside itself. Death forces us to undertake a journey that will lead us far, far away from the life we have always known and, understandably, we yearn to stay where we are, with the people we love. Unfortunately, because of the way the universe is ordered, this is not practical, which is why a funeral procession to the cemetery at Montemonaco always stops and starts and makes frequent random turns and twists—to confuse the ghost. As for the journey back from the graveyard, the mourners always take a completely different route despite the fact that this new route takes them out of their way and is longer. This throws the ghost off course, leaving it with no option but to go toward its rightful destination. Montemonaci also knew that, after a certain point, it's ill-advised to wail and lament since a soul might feel the need to come back and console those whom it has left behind should it hear them weeping and keening.

And that is precisely what happened in the case of our nonna and our father.

Despite everyone's dire warnings, Papa shrieked and wailed and could not be comforted. As a result, Nonna's ghost remained in the environs for the better part of two years, throwing pots and pans, breaking the crockery, slamming doors in the middle of the night, and rearranging furniture. In time she dissipated, dissolving little by little until one day she was utterly gone, but the period had gone down in our family's history as a very difficult time indeed. Emilio had been a toddler when she died; he could not recall the time during which the house had been haunted, but he had heard the stories.

"Who does he think I am?" the Sibyl asked me.

"Our nonna Umbellino," I replied.

"Your nonna? Are you talking about Lucia Umbellino? A most difficult woman. I knew her well." Then, to Emilio, "I am not your grandmother, young man. I am nobody's grandmother, just as I am no man's wife or no child's mother. I am a speaking virgin."

Emilio's jaw dropped. "Are you the…the Virgin Mary?"

"Heavens no! What an idea!"

"It's the Lady Sibylla," I explained.

"The Lady Sibylla?" Emilio was astonished. "If that don't beat all! You weren't blown up then?"

"Mama and I rescued her," I explained. "Last night after everyone had gone to bed."

"Wait until I tell the others!"

"No, Emilio, wait! No, Emilio, you can't tell—"

But he had already managed to catapult himself across the room and out the door. I leapt to my feet and had just started after him when Sibylla cut me short. "Aren't you forgetting something?"

I wheeled around to face the cabinet. "What?"

"The mugwort, child. I may not have a body, but I do have ears and my hearing is preternaturally keen. How that can be, I do not know."

I retrieved the jar of mugwort from the cabinet, closed the door, and headed after Emilio.

As luck had it, however, Papa had collared Emilio just outside of the door. "There you are! I've been looking for you. You're in charge of feeding the donkey and wiping her down. Carmine! Rinardo!" The two younger boys exploded into view. "Help your brother!" Papa let go of Emilio and pushed him in the direction of the donkey. Whooping, the three boys descended upon the terrified donkey and proceeded to swarm her. She, in turn, kicked and brayed.

I tugged at Papa's sleeve. "Emilio knows about Milady!"

"How? Did you tell him?"

"Not me!" I defended myself. "She overheard us and she just started talking!"

"I will instruct them not to say anything. *Boys!*" he yelled.

"Mind that donkey doesn't kick one of you in the head!" Mama warned, as she passed by carrying a big pan of baked pasta. "Is that my mugwort, Mari? I thought I told Concetta to fetch it."

"She was too scared."

"Scared? Scared of what?"

"Never mind. Mama, Emilio knows!"

Mama looked stricken. "Emilio? Addio! Did you tell him? All the angels and saints! Can't anybody keep a secret around here?"

"You told Papa and Concetta! And it wasn't me. She just started talking. Sibylla! She's turning out to be a real chatterbox!"

Mama cupped her hands around her mouth called out to Papa, "Umberto!"

"Don't worry!" Papa called back. "I'm taking care of it." I could not hear what he was saying to my brothers—not at that distance—but from the vigorous way he was flinging his arms around, I suspected that he was threatening them with a series of terrifying punishments should they betray our secret, which would have the effect of silencing them for the hour or so our visitors were expected to linger.

I held out the jar of mugwort. "What do you want me to do with this?"

"Stuff it up the priest's nose."

"What?"

"You heard me. Stuff it up the priest's nose!"

I shuddered. "I don't want to stuff it up the priest's nose!"

"Do you think that *I* want to stuff it up the priest's nose? Trust me, Mariuccia, there is not a person alive that wants to stuff mugwort up that old priest's nose. The question is, is there someone *brave* enough to do it?"

"Oh, all right! Fine! I'll do it!" I marched to the table to where the old man was sitting.

"Tip your head back, Father, and inhale!" Mama shouted her encouragement. "Did you know that John the Baptist wore mugwort shaped into a girdle to protect him from harm in the wilderness?"

Crumbling the dried leaves between my fingers, I took a deep breath and thrust the herb up the old man's vein-riddled beak of a quivering nose.

As was typical for farm families without servants, Concetta and I sat down only long enough to eat one plate's worth of pasta apiece. The rest of the time we spent fetching dishes back and forth to the pergola or serving the men. Then, when everyone looked as though they would burst and the men were visibly woozy with wine drunk under a hot sun, my mother set Concetta and me to cleaning up, while she brought out the mistà. One round of this potent liqueur and Padre Eusebio dug the dried mugwort out of his nose with his handkerchief and announced, "I'm having a nap. I don't care what anyone says!"

"Emilio!" my mother ordered. "Get a blanket and spread it out under the fig tree for Padre! And you, Carmine! Help Padre to his feet!"

Between them, my brothers succeeded in getting Eusebio up, then over to the fig tree, then down onto the blanket, where the old man promptly fell asleep and began to snore.

"I'm feeling kind of sleepy myself," Pasquale muttered, rubbing his eyes.

"Get him a blanket!" Mama instructed me, but before I could return from the house with a blanket, the sacristan's son had gotten up from the table, stumbled drunkenly over to the fig tree and, lying down at the priest's feet, curled himself into a ball and fallen asleep.

After a second round of mistà, Pio yawned mightily, laid his right cheek on the trestle table and fell asleep. A few moments later, the prior joined him. The two men sat slumped, their twitching cheeks flattened against the table's rough surface, snoring, snorting, and muttering. It was a deep sleep that the visitors had fallen into—a mistà sleep, pall like, faintly hallucinogenic, and one from which they would not awaken until the next morning, at which point, with aching heads and stumbling feet, they resumed their journey northward to the Marches.

Concetta mourned their departure, which seemed to her to be the end of something. She was, of course, mistaken. We all were.

Montemonaco is a very small, remote village and strangers a rare sight. The appearance, therefore, of a party of unknown individuals, including an ancient priest on a recalcitrant donkey and a man decked out in an outfit closely resembling that worn by the puppet Pinocchio in the fairy tale…this had not gone unnoticed. Neither had the hollow, reverberant sound of a distant explosion.

Accordingly, less than half an hour after the Castelduranteans' bedraggled and wobbly passage through Montemonaco en route to the valley, a delegation of villagers arrived at our farm determined to discover just what the mysterious strangers had been up to. This delegation was made up of the two most meddlesome and, therefore, most powerful women in the village—Gabriella Favero and Valeria Rossi—and the two men who would have been its mayor and his deputy—had Montemonaco required formal management—Gabriella's husband, Pacifico, and his brother Bruno.

The first Umbellino they encountered was Mama. No sooner did they spot her under the pergola than they crowded around, firing questions from all sides.

"Who were those men?"

"What did they want? Everyone is dying to know."

"Are you all right? There was a big sound, like a clap of thunder, only much louder."

"Who was that man in the funny pants?"

"Was he from Switzerland? It is said that they dress like that in Switzerland."

Mama held up her hand. "Please! Please! If you give me a moment, I will tell you. We Umbellini are fine, thank the Blessed Virgin, but I fear the Grotto delle Fate is not. The Pope himself sent those men to blow it up. And so, they did…blow it up, I mean. That was the loud noise you heard."

There was a moment of shocked silence while everyone attempted to absorb this startling development. Then…

"Blew up the grotto?"

"How could they do that?"

"It's been there since the beginning of time!"

"It's a sacred place!"

"But what about the Oracle?" The women wrung their hands. "Was she…was she blown up too?"

Mama looked uncomfortable. She shrugged. "Who knows? Umberto said that the mountain collapsed in on itself with the force of the blast."

"Umberto saw this?"

"And my sons and Mariuccia too."

"Addio!" Gabriella cried. "What will happen to Montemonaco now? The Lady Sibylla has kept us from harm all these years!"

"She is not our patron saint, Gabriella," Valeria reminded her. "Not like Sant'Agata. We don't pray to the Sibyl."

"When your precious daughter fell ill from the *mal'occhio*, who did you consult? Sant'Agata?"

"I did! I prayed to Sant'Agata for her recovery!"

"And you also visited the Sibyl! You forget that I accompanied you!"

Pacifico intervened. "Calm yourselves. This is no time for splitting hairs. We must assess the damage and determine a course of action—and we must do so quickly if we are to have any chance of saving the Oracle. You return to the village and instruct all able-bodied men to come at once. We will convene here."

Over the next hour the entire male population of Montemonaco began to assemble in our yard—some thirty men and boys, all eager to see with their own eyes the devastation wrought by the Pope's emissaries and their remarkable black gunpowder.

"The faster you dig out the grotto and the sooner the Lady Sibylla is returned to the mountain, the better it will be for all of us!" Mama told Papa.

"How so?" Papa was not a stupid man, but he was unaccustomed to thinking things through and so tended to get mired in the process. Thinking things through, planning, and organization—that was Mama's job.

"If people know that Sibylla is in the cabinet, the men are sure to hem and haw and dawdle. They will say, 'It is too hot for digging. Let's wait for a cooler day.' And by the time they get around to it, it will be October."

Papa considered this. "I could see that happening."

"As for the women, there will be a constant stream of them, all wanting something from the Oracle—favors and spells and advice. That would only wear her out—she is, after all, very old—and it would try all our patience, especially mine."

"Women day and night, traipsing in and out of the house…. On the other hand, they would probably bring us food and drink for our trouble. That would not be so bad."

"And what about our boys, Umberto? You know how they are, always rough-housing. One of them might accidentally break her precious jug, and then where would we be? How could we transport her back to the cave without a container? It would be like your mother all over again, only Milady is immortal."

The evocation of his own recent haunting caused him to shudder. Papa had loved his mother, but putting up with her ghost had taken its toll on him. Was she watching him or not? He could never tell. And all the time complaining and scolding.

"If, on the other hand, everyone thinks the Oracle is trapped inside the mountain, that the matter is urgent, then they will be more likely to apply themselves to the task at hand."

Papa scratched his head. "So, let me get this straight. You want me to—"

"Lie, Umberto, I want you to lie."

So it was that Papa found himself trudging wearily up the goat path to the grotto at the head of a column consisting of every Montemonacian male between the ages of thirteen and eighty capable of self-locomotion, with me taking up the rear.

Despite the advance warning, it was obvious to me that what the men saw on their arrival—an immense pile of rubble entombing what had been as of the day before and, indeed, in perpetuity, a sacred place—shook them to their very core. For a few moments they tried to dissemble. They coughed and turned aside, all the while dabbing at their eyes with dirty neckerchiefs—as if the yellow dust that still filled the air a day after the explosion was the cause of this unmanly display of emotion.

Then, when they had more or less recovered their equilibrium, Pacifico kicked off the discussion. "We know for a fact that the Grotto delle Fate is but one in a vast series of interconnected caverns that extend a very long way underground," he said. "After all, it is well known that, following her quarrel with the Bishop of Campania, the Lady Sibylla traveled all the way from Cumae to Mount Vettore—all completely underground."

While Pacifico was speaking, Papa tugged at the collar of his rough linen shirt and scratched his neck and I could read in his expression how much he longed to tell his fellow Montemonaci that all they need do to find the Oracle was to open the door to his cabinet—so much so that it made him itchy. But he kept his word to Mama, saying, "If I may be so bold as to make an observation, an Oracle is, by definition, one who predicts the future. Therefore, one cannot take an Oracle by surprise—not one that's worth her salt, that is, and we all know that Lady Sibylla is worth her salt and more. This leads me to deduce that she knew in advance of the Pope's plot against her and so took refuge deep inside the mountain in order to ensure her survival."

"Which means that she is down there now!" said Pacifico. "And that it is up to us to dig her out and as quickly as possible."

"Good idea," said Papa. "Let's start first thing tomorrow!"

Pacifico looked aghast. "Tomorrow? Not now?"

"We have to gather up our tools—picks and shovels, wheelbarrows," said Papa. "The women must pack food and drink for us. Tomorrow will come soon enough."

"Tomorrow then!" the men and boys shouted and threw their caps in the air. Having no cap to throw, I turned and ran back down the path toward the farm.

That night there was a party on our farm. It wasn't planned. It just happened.

Not too long after the men left the farm via the goat path to inspect the damage to the grotto, the women and children and those old people who could walk the distance began to filter in, family by family. Curious, not content to wait in the village for the men's return, they wanted to hear for themselves what had happened. However, after an hour or so of telling the story over and over and over again as each new family arrived, Mama's throat grew scratchy. Besides there was dinner to fix, so it fell to Concetta to tell the story.

The women, seeing Mama hard at work under the pergola, remembered that they too, must make dinner for their families. Putting the grandmothers in charge of the younger children, they and the older girls returned to their homes in the village and gathered up whatever was at hand and portable along with an assortment of pots and skillets. Then, followed by a happy troupe of village dogs, they made their way back up the road to the farm where they set the girls to gathering kindling to make other fires, since Mama's cookstove could not accommodate so many.

When the men and boys and I made our way back down the goat path from the grotto, we found the entire farm—from the goat pen to the olive grove, across the yard and around the house and outbuildings to the vineyard—teaming with women, children, dogs, and old people and ablaze with a half a dozen makeshift fires.

The women had tucked pans of baked pasta into the ashes and set meat sauce to simmering in pots hung from hooks over the fires. *Fritti mistos* of brains, artichokes, zucchini, and lamb chops sizzled in cast iron skillets, while on tables drawn from the house and placed here and there were crocks of spelt soup and egg soup and cabbage stewed in wine. In and among these crocks were set plates of stuffed olives and pumpkin tortellini, interspersed with bowls of lentil salad, broad beans cooked with bacon, celery with marrow sauce, fennel with pork liver, and overflowing baskets of fried bread and wedges of flat bread seasoned with rosemary. There was roast rabbit and stuffed pigeons. A pit had been hastily dug in which an entire young pig roasted, dressed with bay leaves, juniper berries, onions, and cloves. And there were sweet things as well: chestnut cake, cheese fritters made with honey, prune dumplings, ricotta pie, and elderflower cake.

"Such a feast cries out for wine!" cried Pacifico. So, the men went home to raid their stocks, not only of green-tinted *verdicchio*, but also of grappa and liqueurs distilled from mountain herbs, and from green anise, and hazelnuts. As for Papa, he sent my brothers to fetch a half-dozen bottles of mistà from the same limestone cave in which Mama aged her cheese.

A free-for-all ensued, with everybody eating everything and even the children partaking of the wine. By the time all had eaten and drunk their fill, and the sun, a round ball the color of a ripe apricot, hovered on a stretch of rosy horizon over the Adriatic Sea, the farm resembled a battlefield littered with bodies of the wounded and dead. Those who had had the foresight to bring blankets lay on them, while others stretched out on the ground or perched on rocks or tabletops. Mothers tended to babies, and old men half-slept under trees, curled up as tight as bony fists. Little children tottered randomly about, stunned, looking like scruffy kittens sideswiped in the road by a cart wheel, until their grandmothers bore down on them and, seizing them by the ear or tucking them under one arm, returned them, scolding, to their respective mothers. In the meantime, their older siblings, exuberant, finding freedom in circumstance, ranged broadly. As for the men, it was as though the alcohol they had consumed had transformed the rocky ground they attempted to negotiate into the rolling deck of a ship on the high sea. Which is to say that the ground seemed to them to pitch and roll, causing them to stagger, teeter, and reel, much to the suppressed hilarity of the children and the consternation of the dogs who moved between them all, eating what they could find or what they could convince someone to give them.

It was then, as the sun was setting and the evening was drawing close about them, that the Montemonaci began to tell stories about the Oracle who had for so many centuries inhabited our mountain and to whose patronage we owed so much. At first the stories were anecdotal in nature and based on personal experience:

"That time the twins nearly died of the ague, she told me how to make plasters out of mustard and flour. It was the plasters that saved them!"

"When my son had that gash in his leg from the scythe—Sibylla advised a salve made of fir balsam pitch and, though everyone said that the leg would have to come off or he would die, he made it through with only a limp."

"What about when that woman from down mountain cast a love spell on my Pepe and Lady Sibylla told me how to break it using the feather of an eagle, an acorn, and the yolk of an egg?"

And the most memorable story of all.

"Do you remember when the *jettatore* came to town?" someone asked.

A hush descended upon the villagers, broken when one of the grandmothers snorted and asked, "The tinker with the eye patch? How could we forget him?"

"Addio! Now that was a terrible thing!" everyone agreed.

"What about it? Tell us about the tinker!" the children cried. Although they knew the story by heart, they never tired of hearing it.

"Umberto Umbellino," someone cried out. "You tell it best!"

"Yes, Umberto tells it best! He shall be our storyteller!"

"Go on, Umberto!"

Papa demurred. "Let someone else tell it. My throat is dry!"

However, his fellow Montemonaci were not to be dissuaded: "Umberto! Umberto! Umberto!"

"Take this to wet your whistle!" Bruno said, uncorking a fresh bottle of wine.

"Oh, all right!" Papa succumbed. "But only because we are here to honor the Oracle of Cumae and this story that I am about to tell of poor Enzo the Tinker speaks to how much she has helped our little village over the centuries." He cleared his throat, took a swig of wine, and began:

"Once upon a time, thirty-seven years ago to be precise, when your parents were your age and I was a boy of eight, along with my friends Pacifico, Bruno, Gian, and Tomaso, a tinker came to town. His name was Enzo and he was passing through on his way to Casteldurante and Fossombrone from Umbertide in far, faraway Umbria beyond the mountains. He was a tall, lanky fellow with big hands and knobby knuckles and enormous feet with splayed toes the size of sausages. I think it's fair to say that Enzo the Tinker had the biggest feet that any of us here in Montemonaco had ever seen.

"How old the tinker might have been no one knew, for,

though his gait was swinging and easy, his hand steady, and his voice unclouded by age, his skin was tanned to leather by a life lived largely outdoors, and his hair, which he wore long and loose, was as gray as gunmetal.

"But the most extraordinary thing about Enzo the Tinker, more extraordinary even than his enormous feet was that, like a pirate, he wore a patch over his left eye and this struck us all as quite remarkable. Now the grownups, your grandmothers and grandfathers, they were polite. They didn't inquire after his patch, believing that to do so would be rude. If Enzo the Tinker wished them to know why he wore the patch, they said, he would tell us.

"The boys of Montemonaco, on the other hand…we were a curious lot and couldn't rest until we knew why. So, one day we asked him, 'Enzo, why do you wear that patch?'

"And he replied, 'Well, when I was a little boy, just a little younger than you, I fell on a stick and put out my eye.'

"And we said, 'We've never seen a gouged-out eye. Please, just lift your patch and show us how it looks.'

"But he shook his head. 'It is too gruesome,' he replied. 'The sight of it would curdle your eyes.'

"Naturally we were not satisfied with his answer. What did he mean by it? Wasn't curdling the magic by which milk became cheese? How were eyes like milk? However, we knew that, if we pressed him, our mothers would cuff us alongside the head for rudeness, so we refrained from pressing him further.

"However, there was one boy among us who was not shy, a very bold boy who would do anything on a dare. His mother was a widow so lost in grief over the death of her husband years before, that in truth, she paid little attention to what her son did, but only doted on him. He could get away with anything."

"Who was the bold boy?" the children wanted to know. "What was his name?"

But Papa only shook his head—as they knew he would. The identity of the bold boy had never been revealed in any recounting of the story they had heard. "That I cannot tell you. That is a very great secret.

"So, we said to the bold boy, 'We dare you to go up to Enzo and tear off his eye patch.' Naturally, he agreed."

"What happened next?"

"Not long after that, on Market Day just as they were closing down for siesta, our gang of boys collected on the church steps to watch while this bold, bold boy snuck up on Enzo, who lay curled, fast asleep, under a tree next to the church. Our hearts were pounding with excitement at the prospect of finding out the truth about the tinker's eye; in addition, we were overcome by guilt—we had neglected to tell the bold boy the potential consequences of looking at Enzo's eye, thinking that this might put him off the dare.

"And right before our eyes he bent over the sleeping tinker and tore off the patch. He had intended to take off running at this point. Instead, he made the mistake of looking into the tinker's naked eye. What he saw mesmerized him; it rooted him to the spot. For, according to the boy, it was not gouged out at all; neither could it be said to look in any way normal. In the first place, it was blue. No one in Montemonaco had ever seen a person with blue eyes before, let alone one brown eye and one blue eye, as was the case with Enzo. But it was not just the eye's color, according to the boy. It was its size and its appearance, for it seemed to be much bigger than his other eye, swollen, straining in its socket, lolling almost. Indeed, according to the boy, it looked more like a blue egg than it did an eye!

"Enzo lurched to his feet, blinking. It was a moment before he realized what had happened, that his patch was gone, but, when he did, he clapped his hand over his blue eye and let out such a howl of despair as I have never heard since." Papa turned to Pacifico and Bruno. "Indeed," he said, "the mere recollection of that howl sends shivers up my spine. The bold boy took off running. As for Enzo, he grabbed the battered leather satchel that he was never without (it contained all his worldly possessions, including the planes and scrops, froes and tongs that were the tools of his trade) and took off at a loping run over the mountain. He was never seen again.

"Over the next several days, two previously healthy babies developed colic, a two-year-old began to vomit continually, and a five-year-old developed such terrible diarrhea that it was all his mother could do to keep him from dying of dehydration. Two nanny goats' and three cows' milk dried completely up, as did the milk of four of the village's nursing mothers. Olive trees withered, fruit spoiled on the tree, and grapes turned black on the vine. As for the bold boy who had torn off the patch and exposed the tinker's eye, guess what happened to him."

"What?" asked the children.

"His poor eyes curdled." Papa nodded. "It happened just like Enzo had warned us it would.

"Obviously for a small village such as Montemonaco so much illness and devastation all at once was a calamity of unprecedented proportions! In the end, the only thing for it was to consult our Oracle. So a group of women, led by my own sainted mother, may she rest in peace…these women made their way up the mountain to the grotto where Lady Sibylla, after quizzing them thoroughly, identified the root cause of all this woe: mal'occhio, the evil eye.

"'What I find strange,' she told the women, 'is that so many and such a range of creation—people, trees, animals—have been affected all at the same time. Usually cases of illness caused by the evil eye are the effect of envy or covetousness on the part of the caster. They occur individually and are unrelated. Is there someone among you whom you know to be envious in nature or covetous? Who are the childless women in Montemonaco? What about someone with blue eyes?'

"When she asked this, everyone in the delegation turned to one another. 'Enzo, the traveling tinker!' they gasped. And they explained what had happened to the bold boy.

"'Well, no wonder!' the Oracle exclaimed. 'The tinker is a jettatore! Whoever and whatever he happened to have passed and so much as glanced at as he fled the village would have been affected by his *jettatura!*'"

"But what's a jettatore?" the children asked Papa. "What is jettatura?"

"A jettatore," Papa explained, "is someone who, without intending to or wanting to, casts the evil eye. He or she is born with this terrible capacity for creating disaster."

The children, who had been elbowing one another with increasing violence during the course of the story, now began to boo, hiss, and hoot. "Bad jettatores! Stone them! Stone them!"

But Mama interceded here. "Stop! Quiet!" she told the children. "You must remember that there are very few jettatores in this world for this one simple reason—as infants they need only gaze upon their mother once and up her milk would dry. This is why baby jettatores rarely thrive and few survive to adulthood. Umberto is not saying that a jettatore isn't to be avoided. No. Of course, you must avoid him. But you must never despise him, for he is the most unfortunate of unfortunates, a true wretch who is wanted nowhere—neither by his family nor in his village nor anywhere else on God's earth. He is forced to wander the world, shunned and feared by all who know his terrible secret."

"That is why Enzo was a traveling tinker," Papa said, "and why he wore the eye patch."

"He was trying to protect us from himself!" Mama told them. "We should be grateful to poor Enzo, not condemn him!"

Chastened, the children settled down to random elbow pokes. "So what happened next?"

"Lady Sibylla gave careful instructions to the women on the old way of curing the evil eye," Papa continued. "If the victim was a tree or a bush, they should throw a whole egg against it. If the victim was an animal, they should collect the spittle of unaffected persons and make the goat or sheep or cow drink it. If the victim was a person, they should pierce a lemon with iron nails and place it under that person's bed."

"This is how we have done it in Montemonaco ever since Enzo the Tinker," Mama said. "In Amandola and Bolzo and

Pretare, they do it the new way, using olive oil and holy water, but the old way works best for us in Montemonaco, and it was the Lady Sibylla who taught us how."

"But what about the bold boy's eyes?" cried the children.

Papa shrugged. "Sometimes there is no cure. This was one of those times. Remember, he had looked directly into the mal'occhio of a jettatore. The Sibyl could not restore his eyesight, but without her intervention, he would have perished. He is lucky to be alive and he knows it."

The stories continued, but, by this time, the Montemonaci were not remembering what had happened within their own lifetimes, but rather stories that their grandparents had told them and their great-grandparents before them.

"Remember how desperate Tarquin the Proud, the last king of the Romans, was to know what had been prophesied about him in the Sibylline Leaves?" someone asked.

The Sibylline Leaves constituted a record of the Lady's utterances that had been written down on palm leaves and bound into nine volumes. Given the fact that there were only ever four Oracles in the world and that the volumes represented the utterances of one, the Sibylline Leaves were as rare as hens' eggs and as precious as rubies. "Tarquin thought that, if he could but know his fate, he might be able to avert it. Provided it was bad, of course. Accordingly, he journeyed to Cumae where he proposed to buy the volumes from the Sibyl. However, he refused to pay the price she set. He declared that it was ruinously high. So she burnt the first three books. When he still refused to pay, she burnt the second three volumes. Finally, in a panic and convinced that, if he did not capitulate, she would burn the final three, he paid the price she had originally set for all nine. He found nothing in these last three volumes concerning himself—only riddles and conundrums regarding some Judaean carpenter. 'Oh,' the Lady said, 'the part about you was in volume 5. Was that what you were looking for?' A sly one, our Lady of Cumae!"

"Did you know she invented the alphabet? What? Well! What do you mean? That's what my grandmother told me!" someone else said.

"Well *my* grandmother told me that, on her way from Campania and before coming to our beautiful mountains, Sibylla stopped off in Norcia, in Umbria. There she lived in a grotto right next to the very lake into which Pontius Pilate is said to have bled to death—the *Lago di Pilato*. Its waters, they say, are tinted red. The Norcians say that it was Lady Sibylla who gave them the recipe for Norcian pork!"

"Marinades? That's nothing!" announced Nonna Benita. "*My* grandmother, a great friend of the Lady Sibylla and her confidante, told me something very, very interesting—scandalous, actually—many years ago. She made me promise not to repeat it."

"What?" Everyone wanted to know.

"I'm sorry," replied Nonna Benita. "I promised not to tell."

"You can't do that!" her audience objected. "Don't be such a tease!"

"A promise is a promise!"

"Well, in that case, who else knows a story?"

Nonna Benita, sensing that she was losing her audience, vacillated. "I suppose it wouldn't hurt to tell just a little bit of what my grandmother told me. Not the entire secret, but just a little."

"What is it then?"

"Well," began Nonna Benita, "It is not only the Lamiae who shape shift. It is also Sibylla. Yes. It's true. On Saturday night she turns into a serpent! And she stays a serpent until the Pope says Mass. But only from the waist down. My grandmother was visiting her when it happened one time. That's how she knew."

"That is not true!" a voice rang out.

Everyone looked around to see from whom the objection had come.

"That is most emphatically *not true!*"

The voice was unfamiliar and the clipped accent distinct, foreign to these parts, more Latinate than the gritty, splayed speech of the upland Marches. It was clear, sharp, and resonant. Indeed, it rang as though it emanated from a jug— which, of course, it did.

Mama's eyes widened in horror. "Sibylla!" she hissed to Papa.

"Shhhh!"

"Emilio?" Mama identified the source of the "shush."

Sure enough, there stood Emilio, flanked by Rinardo and Carmine, cradling the Oracle's jug in his arms. "What?" he demanded. "She made me do it! She did! She wanted to know what everyone was saying about her."

"And it's a good thing I did!" the Sibyl fumed. "Spreading false rumors about me. About *me!* The audacity! The effrontery! No portion of me has ever turned into a snake. And as for that Rosalinda Stracchi woman, she was never my friend.

I have no friends. I have never had friends. I am an Oracle. Oracles do not have *friends*."

There was dead silence for a moment as everyone blinked and shook their heads and looked to their neighbors to see if they had any idea what was going on. Then the Oracle snapped, "What? Will somebody say something? Has the cat got all your tongues?"

Since it was generally agreed that Pacifico was in charge when it came to Montemonaco, he now cleared his throat and began, "Excuse me, but whom am I addressing?"

"The Oracle of Cumae," replied Sibylla magnificently.

This revelation caused the assembled crowd first to gasp and then to mutter, "What? Could it be?" until someone cried out: "Don't you understand? It's the Sibyl! She lives! The explosion did not kill her! Montemonaco is saved! Praise be to all the angels and saints. Thanks be to Heaven!"

"The heavens had nothing to do with it!" Lady Sibylla huffed.

"But, Milady, *where* are you?" Pacifico glanced nervously around, for it seemed to him that the voice emanated not from one specific point but was diffused over a larger area, like something that has melted, spread, and stuck to what it encountered.

"My current residence is a jug," Sibylla informed him. "Emilio, my boy, show these good people my jug."

Emilio raised the jug high over his head for all to see.

"Careful!" Mama cautioned. "Don't break it."

"But, if I may be so bold, *why* are you in a jug?" Pacifico persevered. "Never mind why. How? And how did you come to be here and not buried in rubble inside the mountain?"

"Esperanza and Mariuccia Umbellino rescued me in the dark of last night," the Oracle said, "as well they might, considering all the good that has come to their family because they are my nearest neighbors. And you must forgive them for deceiving you; they were acting on my instructions. As for the story of how I came to be in this jug, it is a long and piteous tale, one guaranteed to illicit both pity and fear. However, seeing that tonight is a night for stories, I think I shall do you the extreme honor of regaling you with it. Emilio, climb up on top of that table so that everyone can hear me."

Emilio did as he was told, and the Sibyl began.

"I was one of the only four genuine Oracles that the world has ever known. There was that girl in Delphi—Pythia, I believe her name was—and that miserable creature in Asia Minor—utterly incomprehensible, that one—and someone in India whose name eludes me at the moment. What has happened to them, I cannot say. We haven't kept in touch. As to how we came to exist, I am unsure. Were we designated Oracles by some great power or created as such? Who knows? I do remember having something like a childhood, but such memories as I retain of that long-ago time are as fleeting and as unsubstantial as shadows cast briefly upon a wall. Perhaps I had a mother and a father and siblings...or were they servants assigned to me because of my great gift? I cannot say. It was a thousand years ago that I was a child and I mean that quite literally.

"One thing I know for sure. I was very good looking—slender and dark with great green globes for eyes and long, silky hair that I wore loosely braided down my back. I was a slip of a thing and as graceful as a young deer with little feet and little hands and whoever it was that dressed me, clothed me in the finest linen, but very simply except for gold bracelets and clasps and earrings. I did not walk so much as dance my way through life. My laughter was like bells chiming, and I smelled better than anyone has a right to smell—like a whole field of flowers. And don't think I didn't know it. Don't think I didn't know it all—every bit of it. Oh, I knew it.

"Given my preferred position as an Oracle and my heart-stopping beauty, it was only natural that a god should fall in love with me. In those days, such things were uncommon, but not impossible. Liaisons between gods and mortals happened. They did. Nobody liked to talk about it...but they did like to talk about it. You know what I mean. However, it was never good for the mortal involved. Never. In fact, it was the end. A moment of blinding ecstasy and then: *poof!* Transformation. One moment you were a pretty girl and the next moment you were, I don't know, a swan, a laurel tree, a constellation. What I'm saying was that there was a price to be paid for being beloved of a god. And it was always paid. It was never *not* paid.

"It was Phoebus Apollo who fell in love with me—the sun god. And not that silly Roman sun god either. Not Helios. He was but a poor cousin to Phoebus Apollo, the Greek god of the sun. Magnificent. Fundamental. If he had been a man, I would have said, 'What a man!' But he was not a man, now was he? No, he was not. He was more. And he was my lord. Because I am a Hellene, after all. A Greek. Cumae was a Greek settlement, an outpost. From Cumae we Greeks spread east and south, throughout the boot of Italy and into Sicilia. But as for me, my home was Cumae and I had the most cunning little cave hollowed out of the rock beneath the acropolis, beneath the temple to Phoebus Apollo and it was there that I prophesied the fates of kings and kingdoms in riddles and conundrums—there that I met with Aeneas and Tarquin and all those other fools.

"Finally, after much flirtation and dalliance, it came down to this: Phoebus Apollo offered me anything if only I would be his. And he was in a position to give me anything, not to mention that he was amazingly good looking, ladies, and, being the sun god, full of fire! We were at the seashore at the time—the Tyrrhenian Sea—and I scooped up a handful of sand and said to him, 'Give me as many birthdays as I hold grains of sand in my hand.'

"'But don't you want eternal youth as well?' he asked, and I…I was young and foolish. I just laughed at him and shook my head and fluttered away down the beach, beautiful as a butterfly, thinking as I bounced along how fetching I must look from behind (for I must advise all of you that, whether going or coming, the view when it came to little me, was always delightful). I was determined to remain a maiden, you see, for no Oracle is not, and besides, I liked myself as I was. I did not wish to turn into a wild boar or a sea urchin. Not for a moment of ecstasy.

"The upshot of all this was that, despite repeated attempts on his part to convince me otherwise, I never surrendered myself to him. I have remained a maiden to this day, if a person without a body can be said to be a maiden. The curious thing was that although I did not grant his wish, he granted mine. He gave me as many years of life as there were grains of sand in that fistful of beach I had scooped up from the seashore. I don't know how many grains of sand there actually were—at least twenty-five hundred, for I am that old and more—but, being a god, I suppose he must have had a pretty good idea. Or perhaps he just came up with a number. Guessed. It is hard to know what a god knows. They play their cards close to their chests.

"As for *why* he granted my wish...that I didn't understand for many, many years. I thought it was because I was his favorite, his darling. I thought it was because I was special. Then, finally, I understood. It was his revenge on me.

"The years came and went, and I grew old and withered and stooped and crabbed—the way all old women do. The difference was that eventually old women die. Death puts an end to their shrinking. But not mine. For me there was no end. And you can only shrink so much, after all. Centuries came and went and, with their passage, I grew smaller and smaller until some nine hundred or so years ago, I disappeared altogether. All except, for my voice."

Lady Sibylla fell silent for a moment, as if overcome with the misery of such an existence. Or, possibly, for effect.

"Go on, Lady!" Mama encouraged her. "We are hanging on your every word!"

"Yes, please! Please go on!" the Montemonaci joined in. "Your story is most fascinating!"

"Ah, well." The Oracle sighed. "If only I had asked for eternal youth to go with my years! If only I had not been so arrogant! True, the fire of a god's touch did not set me ablaze and consume me in an instant of unbearable rapture. Neither was I transformed into a tree or a bird or a star or an estuary. I was not so lucky. I was not so smart. For that would have been the preferred way to go. I see that now—if I can be said to see, but I do, you see. I see each and every one of you. I see the house. I see the wine press. And that is very odd because, of course, I have no eyes. How can I see without eyes? I have no earthly idea. Suffice it to say that I cannot begin to tell you how many times I've kicked myself for not following Apollo's suggestion, for not asking for eternal youth to go with all those years. Metaphorically speaking, of course."

Lady Sibylla paused. It was a poignant pause, soaked in regret. Then she continued, "If I am wise, Montemonaci, and you of all people on earth know that I am, it is a wisdom born of rue. Of remorse, of deepest regret. That is the mother of wisdom—what might have been, what one passed up, what is gone and will never again be. I made a bad choice and as a result, here I am today, a disembodied voice shut up in an old Phoenician jug, at the mercy of men whose understanding of how the universe is ordered is no better than that of termites and swallows. Were it not for you good people— the Umbellini and the Iannazzi and the Stracchi and the Di Nardi and the rest of you, who have, over the years and the centuries, become my people, my *paesani*…"

At this the Oracle, overcome with emotion, broke off, unable to continue. Sniffling and choking sounds emanated from the jug.

We all looked at one another, wondering what we could

possibly do, what in the world we might say that would bring comfort to an Old One.

"Make way! Make way!"

The crowd parted to allow our parish priest of Sant'Agata a passage through. A short, misshapen man in a rumpled cassock, Padre Antonio was thickly built with powerful hands, sparse hair, and eyes that looked like marbles in their thick cataract casings. He carried a cane, so as to better navigate a world that he perceived only as a series of blurred shapes. "Do you recognize me, Milady?" His tone was deferential, his voice soft.

"Is that…is that little Antonio?" the Oracle asked.

"It is!"

"I remember! You were that boy! The one they call 'bold.' The one who stole Enzo the Tinker's eye patch. Oh, but your poor mother was undone! Beside herself. Tell me. Did your eyes ever un-curdle?"

"It's him! It's him!" the children cried. "The bold boy! Padre Antonio is the bold boy!"

The priest shook his head. "No, Milady, they never did."

"But a priest, Antonio? How could you betray me by joining the ranks of those sworn to destroy me?"

Padre Antonio shrugged. "What is a village without a priest? If I hadn't stepped forward, the bishop would have sent a stranger into our midst, someone who did not know our ways, who didn't understand the fealty we owe to you. Before Padre Ignatio died, he and I talked it over. We thought it was a good solution. After all, what kind of farmer would I have made—a blind man? But no matter, Milady, I will always be on your side no matter what, and what I wish to tell you is this: We are deeply honored by your presence among us and look forward to restoring you to your rightful place." At this he executed a clumsy, lopsided bow and shuffled backward.

"Thank you, Antonio," the Oracle said with a catch in her voice. "Thank you, everybody." Then, moments later, once she had recovered herself, "But you know, when I think about it, there really is no pressing reason for me to return to the mountain just yet. After all, I've been a long time underground and it would be good to see the sun and to have some company other than foolish snakes. Perhaps I shall stay the summer or maybe into the fall. Let's play it by ear."

There was a moment of silence, then someone (who knows who it was) began to clap, followed by someone else and someone else. Those who were lying down sat up, and those who were sitting down stood up, and children were hoisted onto shoulders, and babies were held aloft. In a matter of moments everyone in Montemonaco was clapping and cheering and throwing their caps into the air. The dogs were barking excitedly and lunging about, and everyone was crying, "Bravo! Long live the Lady Sibylla! Long live the Oracle of Monte Vettore!"

My mother turned to my father and I saw her mouth the words, "Exactly what I did *not* want to happen! Mark my words. We're in for it now!"

The following day, unbeknownst to anyone else, my mother consulted the Oracle in private regarding a love potion. "I hope you will not take offence, dear Lady, but I wish to bind my eldest daughter to Prior Bacigalupo," she said. "It's probably unnecessary; the man appears smitten. But Montemonaco is far from Casteldurante and, you know—out of sight, out of mind."

"I am astonished that you should wish to form a liaison with the sort of person who goes around blowing up the homes of elderly persons much his superior and whom he does not know," Sibylla said stiffly. Then, "Is he so very rich, then?"

"So it would seem," replied my mother.

The Oracle sighed, "Well, in that case…perhaps your Concetta will make him miserable. That would afford me a degree of comfort. For starters, you'll need some hair from their heads. Hair is essential for a binding spell."

Mama retrieved from her apron pocket a handkerchief folded into four quadrants. She carefully unfolded it, revealing a small lock of oily black hair. "I took the precaution of relieving him of this while he was sleeping off the mistà that first night," she said, feeling rather proud of herself. "Just in case."

"And your daughter's hair?" asked the Oracle.

"I harvested some from her hairbrush."

"Well, then, this is what you must do."

Mama took careful notes, frequently asking the Oracle to repeat herself, especially when it came to the words that she must intone, for these were in Etruscan, a language so ancient that it predated Latin and was understood by no living being.

Late the following Friday night (for the spell to work, it had to be cast on a Friday), and long after everyone in our household had gone to sleep, my mother rose from her and my father's bed. Taking a candle and a flint, she made her way to the oak cabinet, from which she retrieved a stone mortar, her notes, and the rest of the ingredients she had set aside to affect the spell. She stole outside to the pergola. It was a clear night, always good for magic, with a sliver of bright moon dangling as if from a thread in a deep blue, star-spangled sky.

Lighting the candle, she set it on the table next to the oven and peered once again at her notes. She tied the hairs she had plucked from Cesare's head together with those she had retrieved from Concetta's brush. She placed the bundled hairs, a single bay leaf, and a pinch of verbena in the mortar and set the mortar's contents afire with the candle, all the while intoning the proscribed charm: "*Ca suthi nesl amcie titial can l restias cal ca rathsle aperuce n ca thui ceshu lusver etva capuvane caresi carathsle.*"

"I hope my pronunciation wasn't too far off," she worried, then shrugged. "Well, if it was, it's too late now." She stood there in silence for a few moments before wiping the mortar clean, stuffing her notes into her apron pocket, and returning to the farmhouse and my father's rumpled, dream-drenched bed. Little did she know that the hairs she had plucked from Concetta's hairbrush did not in fact belong to her elder daughter, but to an interloper, a thief. In a word—me.

When at length Cesare Bacigalupo arrived at our doorstep a second time, he bore with him many gifts—sugarplums and sweetmeats for my brothers, ribbons and trinkets for Concetta and me, a box of fine cigars for Papa, and for my mother, a black lace mantilla. He wore the same clothes as on his previous trip—black lederhosen, white shirt, red tie, and green felt hat—on the grounds that a man who has come courting must look his best and that the lederhosen not only showed what were, in his opinion, quite shapely calves off to good advantage, but also distracted viewers from the widening midriff that was his secret despair. In his breast pocket nestled a little velvet box containing the diamond ring his father had presented to his mother on their engagement and his grandfather to his grandmother and so forth.

As for what was in his heart, who could say what exactly that was? Shortly after he had left Montemonaco, he had resolved to return and ask for Concetta's hand in marriage. However, for several weeks now, he had been bedeviled by thoughts and dreams not of Concetta, but of her grubby, boyish little sister—of *me*. He knew that this was wrong—in fact, that it was ridiculous! He couldn't so much as remember my name, much less summon an image of my face in his mind. And yet he could not stop thinking about me. Upon setting out on this journey, he had thought to while away the days sorting out exactly what his intentions were—and to whom they were directed. *To get it straight.* Despite his every effort, however, all he had succeeded in doing over the last several days was to further confuse himself, so that by the time he reached Montemonaco, he had no more precise an idea of his heart's desire than when he had left Casteldurante.

Cesare's arrival was greeted by my family with a degree of excitement that bordered on sheer hysteria, fueled by my sister and my parents' burning desire—and their absolute expectation—that the purpose of his journey was to ask for her hand in marriage. My mother had managed to keep the fact that she had cast a spell on the Prior a secret from Concetta, not wishing to raise her hopes unduly or to imply that her charms in and of themselves were insufficient to attract so worthy a swain. But Mama had not lasted a day before confiding in Papa.

The Prior was immediately entreated to join the family for dinner. When he agreed, Concetta and my mother fell to preparing the meal as if they were going to war, ferociously dismembering two rabbits that my father had snared that morning, wedges of onions and fennel and bits of carrots flying in all directions.

While this culinary frenzy was going on, Concetta kept stealing sideways glances over her shoulder at Cesare, who sat with Papa in front of the house. Whenever she happened to catch his eye, she bit her lip and blushed as red as a rose.

As for me, also in the dark as to my mother's recent magical machinations, I dutifully followed her barked instructions, but with considerably less enthusiasm than Concetta. After all (or so I thought), none of this had anything to do with me. Little did I know that Cesare, despite his every effort, was having enormous difficulty keeping his eyes off of me, never mind how very pretty Concetta was and how receptive to his advances she clearly would be.

And it was not only his eyes. His thoughts circled me as incessantly, as compulsively as water circles a drain down which it is being sucked. While Concetta was stealing glances at him, he was stealing glances at me, his hungry eyes devouring my unruly mop of hair, my brown and slightly grainy complexion, the stubbiness of my fingers, the grubby nails bitten to the quick, and the flatness of my chest.

Dinner, when it finally materialized, was so fraught with pent-up emotion and expectation that Cesare at first found himself unable to eat, then horribly unable *not* to eat, with the result that he had to go to the latrine and take off his corset, which he secreted in a nearby hazelnut bush.

Finally, after dinner, Cesare said to Papa, "I say, old fellow, why don't you and I go for a little stroll?" He could not for the life of him understand why he was so nervous. After all, what were the chances Papa would turn down his proposal? None, surely. After all, Cesare was a wealthy man with much to offer. Where in this remote and desert place would there be a suitor who could offer his daughter so much? Retrieving his red handkerchief from his pocket, Cesare mopped his dripping forehead. Why was he sweating so profusely? Why did his hands tremble and his teeth chatter and his bare knees knock? What in Heaven's name was *wrong* with him?

Papa and Mama exchanged a quick conspiratorial glance. She nodded. He smiled. "A fine idea!" my father agreed. "There's quite the view of the valley from just beyond the olive grove. On a clear day, one can see the Adriatic."

"You don't say!" Cesare sounded worried.

My father shrugged. "Today it's a little hazy, but who knows? Maybe we'll get lucky." Tucking a bottle of mistà under his arm and two of the fine cigars the Prior had given him into his pocket, he picked up two glasses and ambled off toward the olive grove in his bow-legged way with Cesare weaving alongside him, looking more stunned than drunk.

When they were out of earshot, I elbowed Concetta. "Your lover is fat!" I hissed. I'm afraid I was a little envious of my sister at that moment. Not because I wanted the Prior for myself, but because I thought she was getting far too much attention.

Concetta flushed angrily. "He is not!"

"Is so! That big belly and those spindly legs! He looks like a giant pigeon." And I imitated Cesare's strut-waddle, feet turned out, chin tucked under, chest thrust out.

Concetta slapped me on the shoulder—once and quickly, so that Mama wouldn't see. "You're just jealous! You're mad at me because you'll never, ever in a thousand years have so fine a suitor as Signor Bacigalupo!"

"I hope I don't! What on earth would I do with such a pompous ass?"

"*Shush!* Enough of that kind of talk!" Mama snapped. "As for you terrible little boys..." Seizing her broom, she brandished it at my brothers. They were engaged in a free-for-all, pummeling one another and shrieking. "If you don't stop this dreadful commotion at once, not even the Queen of Heaven would hold me accountable for what I will do to you!" She rushed into their midst, swinging the broom like a club. The boys scattered, whooping and laughing.

By this time, Cesare and Papa had reached the olive grove. Papa gestured for the Prior to sit on a rock wall, then took his place beside him, placing the bottle of mistà between them. "See!" my father said, pointing to the valley down below. "That is Ascoli Picene and there, to the south, Folignano.

Look! You see that river there? It is the Tronto. And that boil of blue mist? Ah, yes, fine sir, now *that* is the Adriatic Sea."

But Cesare was too distracted to fully appreciate the view. Not only was his belly churning in a faintly menacing way, he had, over the last several minutes, also become aware of a distinct ringing in his ears. This ringing not only made my father sound as though he was speaking to him from the bottom of a deep well, it also made the Prior woozy. It's the altitude, he told himself. But how could that be? He had experienced no such discomfort on either his first trip up Monte Vettore, nor up until that very moment. Determined to equalize the pressure in his ears, he pinched his nostrils and swallowed hard. When this didn't work, he blew his nose. When that didn't work, he tipped his head to the right and proceeded to whack himself just above the left ear with the heel of his hand until his ears popped.

"Yes, my friend," said Papa. "I'd have to say that this splendid panorama is one of my most prized possessions."

"Don't forget your family!" Cesare reminded him. "You have a very fine family."

"That I do, Signor! That I do!"

"And your lovely daughters…I hope you don't mind my asking. Are they by any chance spoken for?"

Papa laughed. "Not as yet, Signor. Plenty of time for that. They are young still."

"But not *too* young?"

My father considered the question. "I suppose not. My beautiful Esperanza was Mariuccia's age when we met and Concetta's when we wed."

"Ah, yes, well!" said Cesare. "Which brings me to my

point." Steeling himself, he mopped his brow once again, took a deep breath, advised his stomach to postpone its acrobatics for at least a while, and turned so that he was facing Papa straight on. "Signor Umbellino, do I have your full attention?"

"Indeed you do!"

"Because I must confess that I was quite struck, the last time I was here, by the beauty of your daughter. So struck—" Cesare could contain himself no longer. The words came out all in a rush. "Well...so struck that I wish to ask for her hand in marriage."

My father feigned astonishment. "I don't know what to say! Excuse me, Signor, but you have taken me by surprise!"

"I hope you do not think me too bold," Cesare pleaded, fearful that Papa might decline his request. After all, who could tell what such a rough fellow might do?

"You must give me a moment to consider your request," Papa informed him gravely. "In the meantime, I could do with another drink. How about you?"

"Please!" replied Cesare, though his stomach was pitching like a ship on a high sea.

My father poured both of them another glass of mistà and the two men drank in silence, Papa gazing down at the valley with an expression so deliberately inscrutable that, try though he might, the Prior found it impossible to read. In truth, of course, my father was cagily biding his time for effect.

Finally Cesare, unable to bear the uncertainty any longer, blurted out, "I know that I am somewhat older than your daughter and that I live at a very great distance, but I am a wealthy man, Signor, an important person. Your daughter would be well provided for, and you would be welcome in my home at any time."

"I do not doubt it," my father said evenly, noting with satisfaction that the Prior was drenched with sweat and vibrating like a tuning fork. However, reasoning that it is one thing to string a suitor along and another to frighten him to death before the knot is tied, he decided to put poor Cesare out of his misery. "And you would make sure that I was well supplied with cigars of this caliber? For I have to say, this is the finest cigar it has ever been my privilege to smoke."

"Of course!" the Prior assured him. "That goes without saying!"

"All right, Signor," my father agreed. "You have my permission to marry my daughter. And now I propose that we join the rest of the family and convey to them our happy news."

We were just finishing up the dishes when the two men wobbled back, looking markedly less steady on their feet than when they had retired three quarters of an hour before.

"Ladies. Your attention, please! You, too, my sons! Gather 'round! I have an important and happy announcement to make." Papa was beaming; we took this as a sign that the desired outcome had been achieved. While the boys crowded in around Mama, Concetta and she exchanged a joyous and triumphant look. Disgusted, I could not repress a snort, but in all the commotion my small expression of contempt went unnoticed.

"A most unexpected development, but none the less welcome for being a surprise, as I'm sure you will agree! As fortune would have it, our illustrious visitor, Signor Bacigalupo from the excellent and most cosmopolitan city of Casteldurante wishes to honor us by more than his presence here today. To make a long story short, he has asked for the hand of our little Concetta in marriage."

Concetta let out a tiny cry of excitement. Forgetting our quarrel, she threw her arms around me and squeezed me so tight I thought she'd break all my ribs. In the meantime, the boys were bouncing up and down and yelping like a pack of dogs at dinner time.

All was not well, however.

"No, no, Signor Umbellino!" Cesare stammered. "You've got it wrong! It's not Concetta I wish to marry. It's—" He turned and looked first at Concetta, then, to my utter horror, at me. It was clear that he couldn't remember my name. "It's that one!" he cried and pointed straight at me.

My father was dumfounded. "*Mariuccia?*"

"Mariuccia? What in Heaven's…?" Mama turned to my father. "Did he say Mariuccia?"

"*Mariuccia?*" cried Concetta. Bursting into noisy tears, she threw her apron up over her face and fled, wailing, in the direction of the olive grove.

Cesare, seeming not to notice the distress his choice of bride had caused, dropped to one knee before me and exclaimed, "Mariuccia Umbellino, will you marry me?" Fumbling in his pocket, he retrieved the box containing his mother's engagement ring, opened it, and thrust it toward me.

There was a moment of stunned silence as we stood

gawking at the ring. It was the most beautiful and rare thing any of us had ever seen. Even the boys went quiet as Cesare removed it from its box and reached for my hand, clearly intending to slip it onto my stubby finger. Jolted out of my temporary reverie by this realization, I snatched my hand away. "No, Signor! Not me! I wouldn't marry you for the all the diamonds in the world!" Catching up my skirts, I fled in the same direction as my sister.

My father looked at my mother, aghast.

She shook her head. "I...I'd better talk to her...them," she said and took off after us.

By the time Mama arrived at the grove, I had taken cover behind the press to avoid being hit by the fistfuls of unripe olives Concetta was hurling at me between accusations. Unripe olives are as hard as buckshot. "He's my suitor!" she shouted now. "You stole his heart on purpose!"

"I did no such thing! I don't even like him! Stop that! *Ouch!* Concetta!"

"Girls! Girls!" Mama implored us.

Concetta wheeled around to face Mama, her hair wild and her face streaked with tears. "Mariuccia stole my suitor! How did she do it? She must be a witch!"

"It's not your sister's fault." Mama put her arm around Concetta and, drawing her close, attempted to smooth her tangled hair. "It's just that...well, there's been some sort of error."

"I'll say!" I declared, standing up and examining my arms. "Just look what you've done! I'm all bruised!"

But Concetta's eyes had narrowed. "What do you mean, *error?*" she demanded of our mother.

Mama looked flustered. "Stay here. And, Concetta, don't throw things at your sister! I've got to check something with Milady. You're not to worry, girls. Everything will be all right." With that, she turned and hurried back toward the house.

"What was that about?" Concetta asked. "And what would Lady Sibylla have to do with it?"

"How would I know?" I plopped myself down on the stone wall. "A pretty sight you are! Sit down." Concetta sat beside me and allowed me to wipe her face with my apron. Despite everything, we were sisters. We fought, but we always made up and we did love one another, just not all the time. "There," I said. "You don't look so crazy now."

"What's Mama doing?" she fretted.

"How should I know?" I examined my upper arms, peppered with small round bruises from the rock-hard olives.

"Mariuccia?"

"What?"

"I need to know. You won't marry him, will you?" She looked so stricken. It was like I might look if one of the goats had died.

I snorted. "Me? Never! I'd rather be dead and in my grave than to marry that ridiculous man!" In light of her evident distress, I added, "No offense." Then, "To tell you the truth, I can't think of a man I *would* want to marry. Maybe I won't marry at all. Maybe I'll just stay on here and take care of the goats when Mama gets too old."

"Don't be crazy," Concetta said. "Every girl wants to get married."

"Not me."

Mama emerged from the house; she was clutching something to her breast. "What's she holding, anyway?" I asked.

Concetta squinted. "It's Milady's jug!"

Suddenly filled with apprehension, I stood. "You don't think…"

"That those two have been up to something?"

"*To magic?*"

Concetta stomped her foot. "She wouldn't dare!"

I wasn't so sure. "You know how she is."

Mama had been known to dabble in magic—with disastrous effects. There had been that time that she had tried to resurrect her favorite nanny goat and its indignant ghost had haunted the upper pasture for the better part of a year, causing the rest of the herd's milk to dry up. Or the time she conjured up a rainstorm, and it rained for three solid weeks, and all the goats got hoof rot.

When she was close enough to see, I gestured toward the jug and mouthed the words, "What is *she* doing here?"

"You know that I can see you perfectly well, Mariuccia," said the Oracle tartly. "Don't ask me how. So there's no use trying to go behind my back because I haven't any."

"What have you been up to, Mama?" Concetta demanded.

"That's no way to speak to your mother!" the Sibyl scolded her. "She was acting on your behalf—so that you would have what you desired."

Concetta ignored her. "What did you do, Mama?"

Our mother sat on the wall, the jug nestled in her lap. "Just a little spell," she said sheepishly. "A little…you know… binding spell."

"*Binding spell?*" cried Concetta.

"You mean a *love* spell?" I demanded.

"Just a teensy one…to ensure that Signor Bacigalupo would not forget Concetta once he returned to Casteldurante. What do you think went wrong, Milady?" she addressed the jug. "Do you think I might have mispronounced the Etruscan part?"

"No, no," replied the Oracle. "If that were the case, the spell would never work. Nobody knows how to pronounce Etruscan and they haven't for a thousand years. And, honestly, Esperanza, I swear by that spell. If done properly, it works every time."

"This is your spell?" I asked the Oracle.

Before she could answer, Concetta burst into angry tears. "What? Am I not pretty enough? Am I not a good enough cook? What makes you think I need *magic* to help me get a husband?"

"Concetta!" Mama warned her, glancing at the jug. "Manners! There's been some mistake, that's all, and we're going to remedy it. Aren't we, Milady?"

Concetta stamped her foot. "Mistake? How can you say that? You made him fall in love with Mariuccia, not me—and she doesn't even like him!"

"First things first," said Milady. "Let's start with the hair. That is the most important ingredient."

"Hair? What are you talking about?" I asked.

"For a binding spell you need six hairs," the Oracle replied. "Three from the man and three from the woman."

"I cut a lock of the Prior's head the night of his arrival," Mama remembered. "Concetta's I took from her hairbrush."

Concetta and I realized immediately what had happened. She let out an anguished howl.

"What? What is it?" Mama cried.

Concetta pointed her finger at me and cried, "It's all Mari's fault! She's forever stealing my hairbrush and when I tell you and Papa about it, you never punish her and now… now she's stolen my suitor." Clearly our temporary truce was over. She hurled herself at me, toppling me off the wall and onto the ground.

Mama wrapped her arms tightly around the jug, twisted to one side and hunched over it so as to protect it from our flailing arms and legs. "Girls! Girls!" she cried.

"Such a display of temper as I have rarely seen in all my thousand years," huffed the Oracle indignantly. "So unlady-like! Continue carrying on this way, Concetta, and I shan't lift a finger to reverse the situation. Metaphorically speaking."

"*How?*" Concetta wailed. "How can you reverse the situation?"

"Think about it," Sibylla replied. "The spell clearly worked. The Prior wasn't the least interested in Mariuccia before; now he can't take his eyes off her. So now we just have to repeat the spell using *your* hair this time. Stop your wailing and give your mother a few strands of your hair. From your head this time."

Concetta fumed, but did as she was told.

"Now, for the Prior," said Mama. She rose, cradling the jug carefully, and made her way back to the house, followed by Concetta and, at a safe distance, me. Stopping before the door, she turned and whispered, "If I know your father's mistà, we should be able to pluck a few hairs from Signor

Bacigalupo's head without his being any the wiser." She pushed open the door and we peeked in.

Cesare sat slumped in his chair, snoring untidily, his mouth ajar, his left cheek flattened against the tabletop. Opposite him sat Papa, also slumped, chin on his chest and a faraway look in his eyes. It was impossible to say whether he was asleep or just in a stupor. A ribbon of drool dangled from one side of his mouth.

Mama laid a finger over her lips, handed me the Oracle's jug, and tiptoed into the house. She retrieved a three-legged stool from the corner, set it down in front of the door, climbed up on it, and reaching over her head, retrieved a pair of scissors from the nail on which they hung. Scissors hung over a door ward off the Evil Eye and keep any potential curses that might come in from outside at bay. Mama stepped off the stool, crept over to the Prior and carefully clipped a lock of hair from the back of his head. This she tucked into her apron pocket, smiling in our direction as she did and mouthing the words, "See? It's going to be all right! I promise!"

"It'd better be!" Concetta muttered to me under her breath. "Or you are going to be in such trouble!"

Of course, in order to work the spell had to be cast on a Friday, and Cesare had arrived in Montemonaco on a Wednesday. For that reason, the rest of us made ourselves scarce the following morning so that my father could speak privately with my would-be suitor.

"When I agreed to your proposal, it was my understanding that it was Concetta whose hand you sought in marriage," he told Cesare. "My wife and I believe that Mariuccia is too young to marry. Therefore, if you want her, you must wait until she is sixteen."

Cesare appeared crestfallen. "That is hard news. However, wait for her I shall, for I love her to distraction, though I can't think why."

To which Papa replied, "If, on the other hand, you do not wish to wait, you are most welcome to have the hand of our dear little Concetta, who, if I may be so bold as to point out, is of an age to marry, far prettier than Mariuccia, and perhaps more to the point, actually seems to like you."

Cesare sighed. "My love clearly despises me, whereas I…I adore each and every hair on her head, unkempt though they may be."

And with that my forlorn suitor and his diamond ring started the long journey back to Casteldurante.

The second spell worked. Well, of course it did. Scarcely a fortnight had passed before my ragtag tangle of brothers espied the Prior's sorry and somewhat bedraggled self once again trudging up the road from Montemonaco, all sweaty and panting. My sister's less than stalwart suitor was clearly unused to so much exercise.

This time it was Concetta before whom he dropped to one knee, Concetta onto whose slender finger he slid the heirloom diamond ring. He made a point of paying little heed to me and once I even overheard him tell Papa and Mama that he could not fathom what had come over him to mistake the object of his fervent desire for her little sister, still so clearly a child and a grubby one at that. Grubby! When he thought no one was looking, however, he would steal furtive and, what seemed to me, longing glances in my direction. I found this all very creepy and kept my distance. I wanted nothing to do with Signor Cesare Bacigalupo and made sure he knew it. This made him, I think, a little sad. At least in light of all that followed, I like to think that it did.

Because of all the confusion over which of their two daughters the Prior would marry and fearful that the Prior might relapse into wanting me—a first spell always being stronger than a subsequent one—Mama and Papa thought it best that the wedding take place as soon as decently possible, that is to say as soon as the banns were read—or, given Padre Antonio's illiteracy, as soon as they were improvised the requisite number of times, which was to say on three successive Sundays. Cesare was sent on his way with instructions to return on the Saturday before the third Sunday, when the wedding would take place, the general consensus being that Sundays were the luckiest day of the week on which to marry, based on what, I have no idea.

Montemonaco was small and remote; of necessity, cousins of varying degrees married other cousins with whom they had probably been playmates. If they were lucky, like my parents, they got along and maybe even grew to love one another over time. Many were betrothed in childhood, which gave them years to adjust to what was going to be their lot in life. Marriages of convenience were the norm; love matches, rare.

Two possible matches for me had been discussed—my second cousin Leo or my third cousin Sebastiano. If Papa married me to Leo, our family would acquire an additional bit of pasturage adjacent to our farm. If he betrothed me to Sebastiano, on the other hand, it would be in exchange for a breeding pair of Lagotto Romagnolo dogs, bred to sniff out truffles.

Of course, I would be asked my opinion when the time came and that opinion would be taken into consideration, but the final decision would be made by my parents, based on a number of different criteria, and I would be expected to go along with it without protest. I liked Leo and Sebastiano well enough but was hardly thrilled at the prospect of marrying either of them. To tell the truth, I didn't see why I had to get married at all. I would much rather have stayed on the farm and taken over the goat herd when the time came. I was never one of those girls who are silly over men.

Concetta's marriage to Cesare Bacigalupo was no less a marriage of convenience—he hoped for sons and heirs; she, for a new and more glamorous life, fine things, a great house, and pretty clothes. She did not love Bacigalupo; she loved the life she imagined he would give her. And that was the way it was. Plain and simple.

But a wedding that lacked what passed for pomp in our village, that was insufficiently lavish in terms of food and drink, would reflect badly on our family. It would suggest that we did not value Concetta, that we thought her unworthy of her suitor's hand. Further it would demonstrate that the Umbellini were not generous, that we lacked in hospitality. And that would never do.

Accordingly, the moment the happy suitor headed down mountain again, bound for Casteldurante, Mama launched into feverish wedding preparations. So much to be done! Every visible surface must be scrubbed and scoured, every corner dusted, every spider web swept away, every object capable of achieving a shine must be polished. The contents of Concetta's dowry chest, all those linens and laces and coverlets and tablecloths that she and Mama had labored over many a long winter night, must be inspected and aired and mended where moths had had their way. A special dress had to be sewn for Concetta—new and white—and a veil of handmade lace—both to symbolize her virginity and, more practically, to ward off evil spirits. The rest of us would wear our own best clothing, which must also be inspected, cleaned, and, if required, repaired; if an outfit no longer fit a growing child, and we were all still growing, it must be let out or a new one made. Food must be prepared and stored. Wine must be bottled. Even the goats came under Mama's ferocious scrutiny. It fell to my brothers to bathe and perfume them and replace the leather thongs around their necks with fresh green ribbons. It was a matter of great pride that Cesare recognize that, although we might be country folk, we could still put on a proper wedding.

Cesare arrived on the Saturday accompanied by Pasquale Assaroti. He was not intended to represent the Bacigalupo contingent, being but the lowly son of a sacristan and an apprentice at Bacigalupo & Son, but rather to manage the donkey, Lucinda, whose job it would be to bear my sister down the mountain to her new home in the valley. We thought this a little odd at the time—that no member of the groom's family or any of his friends would have come along for the purpose of standing up with him. In our naïveté, we did not realize that Cesare was embarrassed by his future in-laws and would rather have his fellow townspeople not know how humble were his bride's origins. And he would have been correct. Looking back on it later, I realized that Concetta's nuptials—what had been for us the result of so much effort and expense—were, in fact, nothing more nor less than a simple country wedding, clumsy and graceless, steeped in tradition and marinated in superstition.

As for the event itself, my memories are scattered and few: Mama tucking a piece of iron in Cesare's pocket to ward off the Evil Eye; a procession to the town square where Concetta and Cesare attempted to saw in half a log using a double-handed ripsaw—an act intended to symbolize how well they would cooperate in marriage and one at which Cesare, who looked like he'd never laid eyes on a saw, failed utterly; the villagers throwing grain at Concetta and Cesare as they left the church, as our people have done since Roman times; and later, back on the farm where the entire village had convened with their tambourines to dance the tarantella or spider dance, so called because it evoked the frenzy of a spider bite victim. Before Cesare's arrival, everyone in the village had been thoroughly schooled in the necessity of keeping the Oracle's continued survival a secret from the man who had officiated over the demolition of her shrine. As for Sibylla herself, her jug waited out the celebration in the same limestone cave where Mama aged her cheese and Papa his mistà.

"I don't know that I could contain myself were I to lay eyes on the knave," she told us. "I'm speaking metaphorically, of course, but it could get ugly fast."

There is one more thing I remember, however, and this I remember with utter clarity. It fact, it has haunted me all my life. It took place at the ceremony's conclusion. As was traditional, my father presented Cesare with a wine glass, which it was his job to hurl at the stone floor of the church. The number of pieces into which it broke was believed to presage how many happy years together the couple would enjoy.

Improbably the wine glass did not shatter when it hit the stone floor, but instead rolled a little way down the aisle and under a pew. When this happened, my father quickly presented Cesare with a second glass, which he did succeed in breaking. However, I could not help but notice as I followed my sister back down the aisle that the first glass, the one that mattered, lay on its side in the dust-clogged place in which it had come to rest, and that it was whole.

Summer ended and autumn began; winter came, closing in around Montemonaco like a tight fist and, with it, a strong Bora—the bitter cold and squally wind that howls in from the mountains of Central Europe on its way to the Mediterranean, bringing with it sleet and snow and, on one dark and raging night in early March, Pasquale Assaroti, soaked to the skin and half frozen. We had had a letter some months before with the news that Concetta was expecting a baby in the spring—most likely in the latter part of April—and now here was Pasquale in the last days of March, whey-faced and grim. It was clear something was wrong.

"What is it, Pasquale?" my mother asked.

He opened his mouth as if to say something, then thought better of it. Instead he removed a packet from under his sodden great coat and handed it to my mother.

She took it from him with trembling fingers. "Addio, Pasquale! Has something happened to our Cetta?"

Pasquale looked distraught. "I cannot say it. Please. Read."

Mama broke the seal on the letter and opened it with difficulty—her hands were shaking. She scanned the first few lines, before throwing the letter down and bursting into tears.

"What is it, Esperanza?" my father cried.

"It's...I..." was all she could manage.

"What is it?" my brothers clamored. "What does the letter say?"

"Read it to us, Mari!" Papa instructed me.

I picked the letter up with trepidation and peered at the spidery, correct handwriting for a moment, trying to get a purchase on its loops and swirls. Then, "Dear Signor Umbellino et familia," I read haltingly, "I am writing to you at the behest of my cousin, Cesare Franceso Adolfo Bacigalupo, Esquire, who is too bereft at the moment to do it himself. I regret to inform you that your daughter, Concetta Umbellino Bacigalupo, died in childbed on this day, March 15, 1821. It would appear that her constitution was not all it was purported to be. On the bright side, your grandson, who is to be named after his father and his grandfather and so forth and so on, that is to say, Cesare Bacigalupo VI, is alive, if not precisely thriving. It appears he was born before his time and, as a consequence, is very small and red and quite unattractive. A wet nurse has been secured for the infant. However, my cousin most earnestly requests that his wife's sister, whose unusual name I cannot for the moment recall, come at once to Casteldurante to assume care of the child, as it is all that I can do to manage the household and, besides, I am a maiden lady and unused to squalling infants. Yours, Antonella Aiello."

I glanced up from the letter, my own eyes filling with tears. My sister was dead at scarcely seventeen and now I would never see her again. The desolation I experienced at her loss was the most profound and intense of my short life and I surrendered myself to it completely. What a sad place our homely farmhouse was that night, dark and cold and full of tears and lamentations! We interrupted our mourning only when the Oracle began indignantly demanding from her jug in the cupboard. "What's going on? Why all the caterwauling? How do you expect me to sleep?"

"Who is that?" Pasquale asked, glancing up.

My father, dashing tears from his eyes, said quickly, "Oh, that is only the ghost of my poor mother, Pasquale. She haunts us, you see." He communicated with a glance to Rinaldo that my brother should straightaway relocate the Oracle to a less public place.

Rinaldo leapt to his feet, strode over to the cupboard, retrieved the jug from it, and scuttled up the ladder to the loft. "*Shhhh!*" we all heard him hiss at the jug, but Pasquale seemed to have believed the lie, for he asked no further questions, but only looked about the room rather nervously in case my grandmother's ghost suddenly materialized.

The following morning my mother and father discussed the matter at great length and, after much back and forth, decided that, if I agreed to the plan, I would return to Casteldurante with Pasquale in two days' time, with my father as chaperone. Once there, Papa would take stock of the situation and, if he deemed it suitable and I wished to stay, he would return home without me.

"It need not be forever," Papa said, patting my arm. "You can come back whenever you want."

"Perhaps you shall meet a fine gentleman in Casteldurante and then you will not have to marry a cousin." Mama sounded hopeful. Lately there had been a number of children born in our village with physical defects—two with cleft palates; one with only three fingers on his right hand; and another with no right hand at all. I had overheard Mama talking with the Oracle about this. Neither of them thought that the Evil Eye alone was responsible for so much havoc.

I did not want to marry a cousin *or* a fine gentleman, but the prospect of going to an actual town, a town *down there*, was very exciting. Up to that point I had never ventured farther from our little village than a dozen miles in any direction, never descended from the oak-clad limestone slopes of Monte Vettore, much less set foot upon the broad, rolling checkerboard of vineyards and olive groves, interspersed with golden squares of wheat, sunflowers, and mustard that comprised my father's "most splendid panorama." Neither had I glimpsed the sea, save as a haze of blue mist stretched along a distant horizon nor seen a body of water larger than a mountain tarn. I had never seen these things nor was I likely to have another such opportunity. And so I agreed to go.

And that was how quickly my life changed course. One day I was a country girl, the next, bound for town. It was a big change and I could not help but be excited. My sister, however, Concetta…she was gone forever.

PART TWO

IT WAS a heady first day of our journey—the steep descent down mountain to Ascoli Picene where Pasquale returned the donkey he had rented from a local farmer, and the three of us—Papa and Pasquale and me—boarded a bright yellow stagecoach bound for Martinsicuro on the Adriatic. My head swam, my heart raced, I was giddy with excitement. But all was not well. As matters fell out, the sudden change in atmospherics proved too great for my montane constitution. Hardy as I was, I had spent my short life at a high altitude and was used to much thinner air than that afforded at sea level. By the time we had reached San Benadetto del Tronto I had fallen ill, by Ancona, dangerously so. That it had sleeted from the time we left Montemonaco until we arrived at the base of the mountain and rained dismally from that point on didn't help. By the morning of the second day, I was so ill that I was past noticing when my father, distressed at my worsening condition, left the stagecoach in Sant'Elpidio a Mare to return home and fetch my mother to Casteldurante so that she might nurse me. "We cannot lose two daughters in so short a time," he told Pasquale.

When at last the yellow stagecoach passed through the old city gate of Casteldurante, three days out from Montemonaco, the sun was setting. I had the feverish impression of a great many very tall buildings all crowded together along narrow winding streets and multitudinous bells clanging Vespers. Then, the coach came to a stop in the Piazza del Liberata. By that time, I was so far gone that Pasquale was forced to lift me, bundled in blankets, out of the vehicle and carry me up the stairs to the front door. In lieu of knocking, he kicked at the big oak door with his boot. It opened. After that I remember nothing.

When next I regained consciousness, it was to find myself sunk deep into a gigantic bed in the middle of a darkened room, which gave the impression, even in the gloom, of being cavernous. At first, I was aware only of my head, which ached and felt as heavy as a melon. After that I must have drifted in and out of consciousness for some time—just how long I couldn't say. Hours? Days?

Sometimes people came into the room. They would check my pulse or lay a cool compress on my forehead before leaving. I thought I heard a woman's voice once or twice, and now and then a baby's cry, but from very far away. For the most part the voices belonged to men—two of them. They spoke in hushed whispers and at first I thought their tongue might be a foreign one, for I could not quite make out what they were saying. However, as time passed and my senses sharpened, I came to realize that the persons in question were speaking Italian, though their dialect was markedly different from my own. Then I heard this.

"Frankly, I can't comprehend what you see in her. Not compared with her sister." A man, whose voice was not familiar to me, followed by one that most certainly was.

"Truly, my dear Pellicola? You do not? I find her utterly captivating!"

Were they talking about *me*? I roused myself. "Signor Bacigalupo?" My tongue felt thick and unwieldy; I was startled at how hoarse and weak my voice sounded.

"Mariuccia! Little one!" Cesare leapt to his feet. "You're awake!"

At the same time, a cool, dry hand lighted on my forehead. "Excellent," the man called Pellicola said crisply. "Her fever has broken. Didn't I tell you that bleeding her to within an inch of her life would do the trick? What do I always say, Cesare? I swear by my leeches!"

"That you do!" agreed my brother-in-law heartily.

"Perhaps our little patient would benefit from some sunshine." Pellicola crossed to a pair of louvred doors and flung them open. Light flooded in, and for the first time I was able to see the great bedroom in which I found myself. Needless to say, it was the finest room I had ever seen, crowded with elegant furniture and boasting a high, vaulted ceiling and a terracotta floor over which lay a sumptuous Turkish carpet.

"There! Now, isn't that better?" He beamed, showing pointy teeth. Dressed in tight buckskin breeches and a camel-colored frock coat, the dapper Dr. Pellicola, whom I guessed to be in his late twenties, had a long, thin face, a receding hairline, and a wispy goatee that appeared just a little askew, as though it might have been pasted on by a tipsy valet. If he found me unappealing, I found him doubly so.

I winced, shielding my eyes with my hand. After abiding so long in darkness, I found the light almost painfully bright. I glanced around. "Where am I? Where's Papa?"

"Why, you're home, dearest Mariuccia! Your *new* home, that is!" Cesare sounded so rapturous it made me uneasy. Had some lingering affection for me blazed afresh now that Concetta was gone? I shuddered. If it had, I was going to have to set him straight and quickly. "As for Signor Umbellino," he continued, "he returned home to fetch Signora Umbellino. But you won't be needing her now, nor him. Not now that you're well. Shall I send them a letter telling them not to come?"

"No, wait!" I was about to say that I wanted nothing more than to see my parents, especially my mother. But then I thought better of it. I was fifteen, after all, practically a grown up, and who would take care of the goats, not to mention my unruly brothers in my parents' absence?

"It's settled then," decided Cesare. "I shall send a letter by Pasquale straightaway."

There was a sharp rap at the door.

Cesare sighed and rolled his eyes at the doctor. "Yes, cousin," he said, affecting patience.

The door opened to reveal a woman in her late twenties

or early thirties with broad shoulders and big feet, judging from the size of her lace-up boots. She was dressed all in black crepe save for a white triangle of a linen shawl trimmed in stiff lace and starched to such an extent that it resembled a porcelain plate through which she had somehow contrived to stick her head. She reminded me of a raven, with her sharp beak of a long nose, her bright insatiable eyes, and that way a crow has of hunching its shoulders and looming. She looked very cross and it was not hard to figure out why. From somewhere down below filtered a baby's high, insistent wail.

"Oh," she said, glancing coldly at me. "She's awake, is she?"

"She is, cousin, Saints be praised!" said Cesare. "Mariuccia, I would like you to meet Antonella Aiello, second cousin to my deceased and much lamented mother. Antonella is so kind as to keep house for me."

Antonella stared icily at me. "I am a poor relation," she said. "If I do not keep house for him, I must retire to a convent and live out my days in poverty and silence."

Unsure as to how best to respond to this, I mumbled, "Pleased to meet you."

"So, Antonella," Cesare asked. "What now?"

The housekeeper scowled. "What do you think, cousin? It's your mewling son. He's crying again."

"Well? He's a baby, isn't he? That's what they do."

She bristled. "And what do you expect *me* to do about it—a maiden lady with no prior acquaintance with any infant whatsoever, *not even one?*"

"Don't ask me. You know full well that I was an only child."

"As was I," reflected Dr. Pellicola a little dreamily. "No, wait. There was a sister, but she ate something in the garden and died. Belladonna, I believe it was. I think I put her up to it, but, as I was only four at the time, I was forgiven. Even then I was fascinated by medicinal herbs!"

Cesare laid a moist hand on mine. "Perhaps you know why babies cry, dear little Mari. You come from a large family."

I dragged my hand out from under his clammy one. I couldn't believe how stupid they all were—not knowing why babies cry. "They cry because they're hungry. Or maybe they want to be rocked. Or because they've soiled themselves and need changing. Does he smell bad?"

Antonella sniffed. "He always stinks. However, I don't think he stinks any worse than usual."

"Then try feeding him."

"There you go," said Cesare heartily. "Hand him over to that wet nurse...whatever her name is. That's why we've hired her, after all. To feed the baby."

Antonella sounded faintly triumphant. "Her name is Flora and her contract is for six feedings a day. No more. No less. She has fulfilled the terms of her contract for today and so she's left."

"*Wah-wah-wah!*" wailed the baby. "*Wah!*" One thing you could say for that first little Cico—he had a pair of lungs on him.

I winced. "Surely you have a pap boat!"

"Well, yes," said Antonella, her nose wrinkling. "But you can't expect *me* to feed him. In the first place, I don't know how. In the second place, he is neither my concern nor my responsibility." She glared at Cesare. "I told you that from the outset, cousin. I am a housekeeper, not a nanny."

I could scarcely believe what a fuss she was making over feeding a baby. Commandeering my meager supply of strength, I struggled up onto my elbows amid the heap of bedclothes and pillows. "Bring him to me and I shall feed him."

"But you are unwell, my dearest!" Cesare was all solicitude. "Do you think you are strong enough for such an undertaking?"

"Strong enough to hold a baby? I should think so! Just prop me up on some pillows, will you?"

Cesare dove for the bed with more zeal than I had anticipated, pried me off the mattress and crammed pillows behind my back. "I'll thank you to keep your hands to yourself!" I snapped, for it seemed to me that, in the process of propping me up, he had managed to touch me distinctly more than was necessary.

Pellicola turned to the housekeeper. "Please bring Signorina Umbellino the baby and the required contrivance and stop causing so much trouble."

Antonella's face flushed scarlet and she glowered fiercely at the doctor, before turning on her heel and loudly stomping off.

"I see that Antonella is still skittish about entering this room," Dr. Pellicola said to Cesare.

"She refuses to cross so much as the threshold," Cesare replied. "It's most inconvenient."

The doctor made a clicking noise with his tongue and shook his head. "How many years has it been?"

"Three this March," replied Cesare.

"Three years since what?" I demanded. "What are you talking about?"

"Three years since my mother died," Cesare replied. "She died here, in this room. Well, it was her bedroom, after all. Antonella was with her at the time. She's never gotten over it. She swears my mother's ghost haunts this room, that she has spoken to her, accusing her of dreadful things. So now she refuses to step foot in here. On principle. Have you ever heard anything more ridiculous?"

"My grandmother's ghost haunted our house," I said.

Cesare and Dr. Pellicola thought this was hilarious. They laughed and laughed. Finally, gasping for air and wiping tears from his eyes, Cesare patted my hand. "How charming you are with your primitive unscientific notions! Isn't she charming, Pellicola?"

"She's all right," replied the doctor mildly.

"You mustn't let poor Antonella spook you," Cesare advised. "She had a very...complicated relationship with my mother and her death...well, I think it unhinged her just the teensiest bit. Hearing voices. You know."

"Don't forget that Antonella's had you to herself over the last three years," Pellicola reminded him. "Remember how threatened she was when you brought Concetta home? Doubtless she is disappointed that Signorina Umbellino's ague turned out not so bad as to be fatal."

Cesare sighed. "You're undoubtedly right. But just wait. I'm sure Mari will win her over given time, for who could resist her?"

Antonella returned with the pap boat. Sure enough, she

came no farther into the room than the lintel of the door, but instead handed Cesare the contrivance, which he then handed to me. It was by far and away the fanciest pap boat I had ever seen. In Montemonaco these were typically sewn of leather or carved from bone; this was made of majolica. It was a vessel similar in shape to a gravy boat, with a lip at one end that could be inserted into a baby's mouth. I had used a pap boat to feed orphaned baby goats and occasionally a baby brother if Mama was busy or away. While I was testing the temperature of the pap, the housekeeper withdrew, returning a few moments later with Cico, swaddled to within an inch of his life and shrieking like a banshee. "Here!" She thrust him toward Cesare like a bundle of dirty linen. "Take him!"

"For Heaven's sake, you've got to support his head!" I said. "He's a baby, not a ham!" The housekeeper took a step backward into the hall, wiping the palms of her hands on her flanks.

"Now I can get to my own work! Finally!" Reaching forward, she seized the doorknob and pulled the door shut just loudly enough to make her point.

I sank back against the pillows and carefully unpeeled a layer of damp blanket from around a very small, very red face, slick with tears and mucus. Through his wrappings I could feel how tiny and shrunken he was—far more so than any of my brothers at his age. I remembered that he had been premature by at least a month. "Don't worry, little nephew," I whispered. "We'll fatten you up." Taking a corner of blanket, I gently dried his face. Two little eyes peered solemnly back at me. The baby hiccuped, then sneezed, then smiled.

"Look!" Cesare cried. "He smiled! His very first smile!"

"Actually, I am told that babies don't really smile until about the age of two months," said Pellicola drily. "It's probably just gas."

Cesare did not appear to hear him. He beamed at me; his joy patent. "Cico's very first smile, Mariuccia, and for you! What do you think of that?" He turned to Pellicola. "What did I tell you? No one can resist her. Not me and certainly not our little Cico! It's just as I hoped! He will not lack for a mother, for he will have Mariuccia!"

I frowned. "I am his *aunt*," I corrected Cesare. "Concetta was his mother." Dipping my finger into the warm pap, I slid it into Cico's tiny mouth. He sucked on it eagerly. I could feel the delicate ridges of his hard palate, his toothless gums. And then it struck me, as hard as any blow. This baby was half Concetta's and now she was gone. Cico might not be of my flesh, but he was of my blood and I would do everything within my power to keep him safe from harm. Emotion overpowered me—some combination of despair and love. Tears welled up in my eyes and began to make their way down my cheeks.

"Do I see tears?" Cesare leaned over me, solicitous. "What is it, sweet girl?" His breath smelled like garlic and cigars.

"Back off! I'm all right. Just thinking about my sister."

Cesare straightened up. "Her sister!" He turned to Pellicola. "Her dear, departed sister! Is this girl not tenderhearted? Is she not an angel?"

Pellicola sighed. "Really, Bacigalupo, sometimes you are too much even for me." He picked up a shiny top hat and his doctor's black bag. "Make sure Antonella does not overburden our patient with the infant's care for the next little while.

The fever has left her weak and she could relapse if overtaxed." He glanced around. "Well then, I'll be on my way. Signorina Umbellino, it was a pleasure to meet you." He gave me a little bow, which I acknowledged with a nod. He left, closing the big oak door behind him.

Cesare produced a handkerchief from his pocket and handed it to me. I wiped my eyes and blew my nose and, rather rudely I fear, handed it back to him. I was beyond caring. I turned my attention to Cico, who was sucking ardently away on my finger, all the while staring at me with what appeared to be frank adoration. Poor little mite, he looked absolutely starved for love. I hoped that the wet nurse had cuddled him even a little during his feedings; it was clear Antonella would not have deigned to touch him one whit more than absolutely necessary. Babies need to be held; otherwise they will not thrive. I withdrew my finger from his mouth. He wriggled and cooed. Again, the tiny smile. I poured a little pap into the boat, inserted the lip of it into his mouth, and tipped the vessel just enough that he could take in the mixture without it flowing all over his face. In no time at all, he was fast asleep.

I looked up to see Cesare, perched at the end of the bed, staring at me with his big St. Bernard dog eyes. It made my skin crawl.

"What?" I said.

"He likes you."

"Yes, well, he's a baby. Babies like people who are kind to them."

"I like you too."

I did not care for how that sounded; neither did I like the look on his face—amorous, but also somehow calculating.

"You are my sister's husband," I said flatly. "My brother-in-law. I suppose you are all right as those things go."

"Do you remember that I liked you first?" he asked. "Before your sister?"

"I do," I replied. "But then you came to your senses."

"Did I?"

I met his gaze squarely. I have faced off against billy goats more menacing than Cesare Bacigalupo and put them in their place with a swift knee to the chin. "You did. And that's the last I want to hear of this. Now take Cico and put him in his bassinet. I am tired and need to sleep." It was true; suddenly I felt exhausted. Cesare bent down to take the baby and, while in position, tried to plant a kiss on the top of my head, an effort I foiled by ducking.

"Very well, then," he grumbled, straightening up, doubtlessly feeling as foolish as he looked. "Get some sleep, little Mari. Ring the bell if you need anything."

He left, looking dejected and shut the door behind him. I listened to his footsteps in the hall, then, moments later, to the sound of someone heavily descending stairs.

I glanced about the room. On the wall hung a portrait of a cranky looking woman with a high forehead, pinched expression, and several double chins. Was this Cesare's mother, the woman who had died in this room and whose haunt this was?

I closed my eyes and tried to feel her presence; in my nonna's case, you could sense she was there even on those rare occasions she fell silent—strongly to start off with, then, as time wore on, less and less. It was hard to say for sure. In any case, I was not overly concerned. Ghosts only bother those with whom they have had dealings in life; they do not form new relationships. And, besides, the world is crammed with ghosts; they are everywhere. There's no avoiding them and you are a fool to try.

The living, however…they are another matter.

I sat up and, with some difficulty, pushed the heavy coverlet to one side. I slid to the edge of the bed. It was very high—so high that my toes dangled a few inches above the floor. Carefully I dropped over its side and onto the cold tile. My knees crumpled a little beneath me and a wave of dizziness swept over me. I clung to the bedclothes until the sensation passed. Then, mustering what strength the ague had not sapped from me, I set off across the floor, taking the distance one wobbly step at a time until I finally made it to the door and turned the key, locking the door from the inside.

I was to do this every night in the days to come and a good thing too, for every night after Antonella had finally skulked off to bed, Cesare came scratching at my door like a cat, imploring me to please, please let him in, for he loved me to such an extent that he was plainly dying of it and, seeing that this was the case, how could I be so unkind as to refuse him?

I responded to this by telling him to go away and leave me alone, that I did not love him and never would. This would go on for up to a half an hour some nights and generally ended with me putting a pillow over my head and pretending to be asleep.

By the following morning, I was feeling much better, and as the weather was fine and the sun shining, I asked Antonella if I couldn't get some air. I was unused to being cooped up for so long and longed to be outside.

The housekeeper muttered and grumbled but sent a boy to consult with Dr. Pellicola. He must have replied in the affirmative, for it was not long afterward that Flora, the bustling, snappish wet nurse, brought me Cico, then, complaining that attending on me was not in her contract, bundled us both up in blankets and deposited us in a curious sort of chair on the balcony. The chair had two blades fitted onto the ends of its legs like the rockers on a cradle. When I told her I had never seen such a marvelous chair, she exclaimed with indignation, "What heathenish backwater do you come from that they don't have rocking chairs?"

That morning gave me my first real glimpse of Casteldurante, or at any rate, of the piazza onto which the house fronted, and I watched with great interest as black-veiled, bare-footed Poor Clares, whose convent was just one door down, picked their way across the cobblestoned expanse. Men with polished boots and pomaded hair emerged from the narrow streets that converged to form the piazza and checked their gold pocket watches. Now and then, passersby would let their gaze stray my way and catch my eye; some even nodded or raised a hand in brief greeting. I did not know it then, but I was something of a curiosity in Casteldurante—the younger sister of that poor little wife of the eminent manufacturer

Cesare Bacigalupo—you know, the pretty girl from the country who had died in childbirth just weeks before. So tragic!

Later, after Flora had helped me back to bed, Antonella stuck her head in the door to see if I needed anything.

"Flora is very cross about having to help me," I told her. "She says that's your job, but you refuse come into this bedroom. Why is that?"

She stiffened. "Someone died in this room."

"For the most part that's what people do," I said. "Die in rooms, I mean. I suppose the odd one dies outside. You can't stop going into a room just because somebody dies in it. You'd have to stay outside all the time if that were the case."

"It's not just that someone died in this room," she said. "It's that one person *in particular* did."

"Cesare's mother?"

She nodded.

I pointed to the portrait. "Is that her?"

She nodded again.

"What was special about her?"

"She wasn't special," Antonella corrected me. "She was particular. Particularly awful!" Then she grinned. It was the first smile I had seen from her; it lit up her face like a candle does a cupped hand, but only for an instant. The next minute she was scowling again. "We didn't get along."

"Cesare seems to think you did. He says you've never gotten over her death."

She snorted. "Well, he's right about that, but not because there was any love lost between us. She was intolerably cruel to me."

"Why then? I should think you'd be glad to be rid of her."

THE ORACLE OF CUMAE

"I was. But it's more complicated than that."

I pulled up the covers to my chin. "What do you mean?"

Antonella slouched against the lintel, at ease for the moment. "It was first thing on a Monday morning. I was over there at the vanity, brushing out her hair—she had long gray hair that reached to the back of her knees. She was so proud of that hair. Had never cut it." She shook her head. "A vain, stupid woman. I thought it made her look like a witch, an old, mean witch…that was what she was. At first she complained of tingling and numbness, then of a creeping cold beginning in her toes and fingers and moving inwards. She began to sweat, all the time saying that she was cold, Antonella, so very cold and why was it so dark all of a sudden and could I speak up, she could hardly hear me. I got her to her bed—she was shaking like a leaf and pale! Her eyes were sunken, and their whites looked like hard-boiled eggs that have gone off—slick and thick and white, but also slightly green, you know?"

Antonella glanced at me. I nodded.

"I ran to fetch Cesare and he set out straightaway for Dr. Pellicola. I came back upstairs. I didn't want to see her. Not then, not ever. But I came back anyway and stood where I am standing now, in the doorway. 'Antonella!' (And her voice was so weak; she croaked like a frog.) 'Antonella, you wretched creature! You ugly girl! I am dying! Come here and comfort me!' And she held her arms out to me, pleading. I stood like so." The housekeeper widened her stance, straightened up, and crossed her arms over her chest. "I stood my ground, didn't budge. 'Do you not hear me?' she cried. 'I am calling for you, you useless creature, you parasite! Come here!' I

shook my head. 'If you don't come here right now and comfort me, you shall never be rid of me! I shall haunt you for the
rest of your days!' I turned then and started down the stairs. 'I
know what you have done!' she shouted after me as the front
door opened and Cesare and Dr. Pellicola arrived.

"'Murderess!'" Antonella paused for a moment, then
repeated the word, more softly this time, "'Murderess!'" She
fell silent for a moment, then blinked. "And that was the last
thing she said to me. To anyone, for that matter. By the time
Cesare and Dr. Pellicola had made it up the stairs, she had
fallen into a deep swoon from which she never awoke. She
died an hour later."

"She thought you murdered her?" I asked. "How?"

"Poison, I expect," replied Antonella. "She was always
complaining about the food."

"What did the doctor say she died of?"

Antonella shrugged. "He couldn't say. It's a mystery."

"And now you think she haunts this room?"

"I don't think it. I know it. And I know Cousin Cesare
and Dr. Pellicola say I'm being silly and superstitious, but
Cousin Lucretia is *here*. She is. I know it. And I'm not going
to give her the satisfaction of taunting me from beyond the
grave. I'm not. She did that all my life and, now that she's
dead, I won't tolerate it. As long as I don't pass beyond this
door, I am free of her. The moment I step inside the room,
there she is, inside my head, berating and scolding me."

I reflected on this. "My nonna haunted our house, but
only for a year or so. It was because my Papa missed her too
much; he couldn't let her go and so she stayed. Eventually she
went away. There was gradually less and less of her and then

she was gone. Three years is a long time. Your cousin Lucretia may be long gone by now."

"Not her," said Antonella grimly. "Your father's love for his mother tied her to life; my hatred for my cousin binds her to me and hatred is more powerful than love, more enduring."

We remained silent for a moment, as I considered Antonella's story, then the housekeeper, doubtless regretting the degree to which she had opened up to a stranger, cleared her throat and shook her head and said with icy formality, "If that will be all…"

It became my custom during my recuperation to spend several hours each day sitting on the balcony and observing what was—to me—the exotic life on the piazza. That was what I was doing when I spotted Pasquale Assaroti at the opposite end of the piazza. It had been more than a week since Cesare had dispatched him to Montemonaco with a letter to my parents advising them of my improved health and here he was at last, returned from the South, perhaps with a letter for me…or so I hoped. "Pasquale!" I cried, waving vigorously. "Pasquale, up here!"

He spotted me on the balcony, lifted a hand in greeting and hurried across the expanse of cobblestones, coming to a halt just below the balcony. "Hallo, Miss! Feeling better?" he called up. His rough clothes were red with road dust and he carried in his right hand the handle of a battered leather satchel that looked strangely familiar.

"Did you see my family?" I cried excitedly. "Is there a letter for me?"

"There is and your mother sent you this." He hefted up the satchel, which I now recognized as belonging to Mama.

"What's in it?"

"Dunno. It's a secret. She told me if I were to open it, I would die a thousand horrible deaths, so I didn't. Open it, that is."

"Come up," I wondered what secret the satchel could possibly contain. "Come up at once!" I rose and went into the bedroom.

There was the sound of commotion downstairs—Flora colliding with Pasquale in the hall. Cico must have finished his feeding; she would be returning him to my care.

"What are you doing here?" I heard Flora demand crossly. "No one ever tell you about knocking?"

"Miss told me to come up!"

"Well, up with you then, but mind those muddy boots, or that gorgon of a housekeeper will turn you into a stone statue of your former self!" A moment later Flora rapped at my door, then opened it without waiting for a reply. "Here's Pasquale to see you." She raised her eyebrows archly and glanced back over her shoulder at the sacristan's son. As if I cared a fig for the spotty likes of Pasquale Assaroti!

"Let him in. He's got a letter from my family. And something else besides. You stay." I was alone in the house except for Flora and Cico—Antonella was at the butcher's and Cesare was still at the factory. I didn't want anyone telling tales out of school, especially Flora who had a tongue on her like a prickly pear and a mind that never strayed far from the gutter.

At the sound of my voice, Cico's tiny face crumpled and turned the color of a plum; he began to sputter, tears squirting out in all directions.

"What is *wrong* with this child?" Flora demanded, glaring down at him.

I sighed. I was fond of Cico. Of course, I was. How can you not love an infant, especially one who clearly adores you? The fact that he left off wailing and grizzling only when I held him, however, was beginning to wear thin. "Just give him to me, Flora. I seem to be the only person in the world he actually likes." The instant Flora handed him to me, Cico quieted and began, instead, to wriggle and coo. Remarkable. Annoying. "Yes, yes," I told him. "I see you. Yes, I do. Now, hush for a second." I turned to Pasquale. "My letter?"

Pasquale set the satchel down on the bed and, reaching inside his coat, he removed a piece of paper folded in thirds and sealed with wax. He handed it to me. I broke the seal and scanned the words written in Mama's rough hand:

> *Dear Mariuccia,*
> *We are all well here and happy to hear of your*
> *recovery. The goats and the boys are doing fine. How*
> *is our grandson? We are eager to hear word of him.*
> *I have sent you some cheese and mugwort and also a*
> *little something extra. You will know what it is when*
> *you open it. Be careful. If it breaks, there will be Hell*
> *to pay. Between you and me, the situation here was*
> *becoming intolerable, what with the women of the*
> *village dropping in at all hours of the day or night*
> *and, besides, she wanted to get out and about a little,*

see something of the countryside. It seemed like a good opportunity. We expect to have the grotto dug out by summer's end. She can return then.

Love, Mama.

"It smells funny," said Pasquale. "The satchel."

Stunned, I said, "That'll be the cheese."

"Cheese?" Pasquale was disappointed. "Is that what's in there—cheese?"

"And mugwort," I managed, itching to get at the satchel. Had Mama really dispatched the Oracle to Casteldurante *in a satchel?*

"She told me that I would die a thousand horrible deaths." Pasquale was indignant.

"She didn't want you to eat the cheese," I said. "It's very good cheese. One bite and you would have eaten the whole thing. You couldn't have helped yourself."

"Still!"

I needed them to leave. I rallied myself. "Thank you, Pasquale. Thank you, Flora. That will be all."

"Right!" said Flora. She looked at Pasquale, who seemed reluctant to go without seeing for himself the contents of the satchel he had been charged with carrying for the entire return trip from Montemonaco. "Well, what are you waiting for?" she demanded. "You've done what you came here to do. Get along with you now." She turned to me. "Right. I'll be back at Vespers and not a moment sooner! The little ingrate!"

They both left. I closed the door behind them and leaned my back against it, staring at the satchel, waiting until I heard the front door close behind Pasquale and the back door behind Flora. Then I deposited a protesting Cico in his bassinet and, returning to the bed, opened the satchel and retrieved from it an object wrapped in a flour sack and tied up with string. I untied the string and peeled away the coarse sackcloth to reveal the squat amber jug with the turquoise handle.

"Cat got your tongue?" Sibylla's voice crackled from the jug. "Put me somewhere, *anywhere*, as long as it's far away from that terrible cheese! Four days of solitary confinement with a Caprino di Montemonaco half again as big as my jug! What was your mother thinking of?"

I glanced around the room, looking for a place to set the jug down, but the Oracle preempted me. "Over there by the bed will do nicely. By Zeus, that cheese stinks! And that mugwort was no picnic, either! I'll tell you that!"

"Milady, keep your voice down!" I pleaded. "Antonella will be home any minute."

"And who is this Antonella? Now, this is what I call a pleasant room, Mariuccia Umbellino! So airy! Really, my dear, your father's house could do with a few more windows!"

"Monte Vettore is cold in the winters. Would you like us all to freeze? And Antonella is the housekeeper."

"The housekeeper? A slave? I don't give a drachma what a slave thinks. No, nor an obol either."

What was she talking about? Drachmas? Obols? "She's not a slave."

Sibylla ignored me. "Well, now that the journey is over, I'm glad I made it. I haven't been away from my mountain for more than a thousand years and I wanted to see what's become of the low country. My old home of Campania was such a land as this, albeit on the other side of the Appenines and on the sea. That is to say, it was *low.*" Clearly, living among people had made the Oracle more talkative than previously.

"Really, Milady, try to keep your voice down. You're not among friends here!"

"And that's the other thing," said Sibylla. "A little matter called revenge. I'm not going to lie to you, Mariuccia Umbellino, I wanted see for myself this prior—the one who blew up my cavern—and determine how best to punish him for his transgression."

I considered this for a moment. *What,* I asked myself, *would Mama say?* "Well," I began, "Cesare is the father of my nephew and we must think of what is best for Cico. On the other hand…" I trailed off, trying to find the words to delicately convey what my brother-in-law had been up to every night since my fever had broken.

"Yes?" said the Oracle. "And?"

"He's been acting weirdly, like he did when he first came back to Montemonaco and asked Papa for my hand instead of Concetta's," I told her.

"Has he…"

I shook my head, feeling my cheeks flush with embarrassment. If you are raised on a farm, you have no need to be told how new life is created; that doesn't mean you talk openly about it. "No," I assured her. "But only because I lock the door every night straightaway after Vespers. Even then he comes to the door and begs and pleads to be let in. It's annoying, but it's scary too. What happens if he takes the key and I can't lock the door? I can't for the life of me understand why he hasn't thought of that before now."

"Not very bright, is he?"

"A total idiot. What I don't understand is why he's acting this way—like he's in love with me. You and Mama recast the spell. It worked. He married Concetta."

"Well, *I* understand," the Oracle said tartly. "It's a simple case of overlay. When we recast the spell, we didn't *remove* his infatuation with you, we simply overlaid it with a spell that bound him with Concetta. Now that Concetta is gone—"

"I thought you two knew what you were doing!"

"Don't be impertinent, girl! How were we to know that Concetta would die so young? She seemed healthy enough. Anyway, it's impossible to extinguish love once it is ignited by magic. And, by the way, if you're wondering why that baby so dotes on you, it's because love that results from sorcery is passed on down the line. It's in the blood. All Cesare's descendants will adore you. Treat them badly. Beat them. Do them grave wrong. They will still love you. They will not be able to help themselves, no matter what. I'm afraid there's no getting around it. We will simply have to find someone else for the Prior to fall in love with. Unless of course, we kill him, which would solve the problem once and for all."

From down below I heard the sound of the back door opening and closing. Antonella had returned. "It's the housekeeper!" I told the Oracle. "I have to hide you!"

"Stuff and nonsense! You'll do no such thing. I'm done with hiding."

"But she'll notice your jug!"

"Tell her that your mother sent my jug to you—as a gift. To remind you of home. As a cherished antique. I don't care what you tell her. You'll think of something."

We heard the sound of Antonella climbing the stairs, followed by a sharp rap on my door. Without waiting for an answer, she opened the door halfway and stuck her head in. "I'm back," she announced. "Do you need anything?" Then she spotted the jug. She opened the door all the way and placed her hands on her hips. "And *what*, pray tell, is *that?*" Her tone was icy, her expression, that of someone who discovers a dead mouse in her soup…and, admittedly, in the light of day, in this well-appointed bedroom, the Oracle's repository looked impossibly antique, like some artifact from the lost City of Atlantis, washed ashore tangled in seaweed.

"That? You mean, that?" I pointed to the jug, trying to buy time until I could come up with a plausible explanation. "It's a…a…it's an old family heirloom. Been in the family since Roman times. My mother sent it to me. Pasquale brought it. He brought a letter too. You just missed him."

But Antonella was not to be diverted. "It looks dirty," she said.

"It's old."

"Is it sanitary?"

"Of course it's sanitary! That is, we wash it from time to time."

"It had better not leave a mark on that marble top. Do you know how hard it is to remove a stain from marble?"

"There will be no stain."

"There had better not be. Right then." She left, closing the door behind her.

"The nerve!" the Oracle exploded. "Old? Unsanitary? Who does that slave think she is? With whom does she think she's dealing?"

"Shhh!" I tried to shush her. "She's not a slave. She's a housekeeper, and you mustn't let her trouble you. She is a rude, ignorant woman, unworthy of your notice."

"But how can I, one of only four Speaking Virgins that the world has ever known, allow myself to be insulted like that?"

"But what can you do about it, Milady. You're in a jug!"

"Oh, you'd be surprised what you can accomplish in a jug!"

I sighed and kneaded my forehead. "Please, Milady, let it go. We have bigger fish to fry than Cesare's snippy housekeeper. We need to find Cesare a new object of desire before he...well, you know."

"Well, don't ask me who to enchant! I don't know anybody in this town."

"The only woman I know is Flora the wet nurse," I said, "but she's already married."

I sat there for a few moments racking my brains, then suddenly, "I've got it!"

This from the jug.

"Got what?"

"What do you think? A new object of desire for the Prior! She's *perfect!* Absolutely perfect!"

"*Who?*"

"The slave!"

I stared at the jug. "You mean *the housekeeper?*"

"Yes, that's the one! You know! What's her name?"

"Antonella?"

"*Antonella!* Yes, that's exactly who I mean!"

The following day, Antonella knocked on my bedroom door. She carried a covered wicker basket over one arm. "There's the marketing to do," she announced, "so, if you need anything, there's no point calling for me because I won't be there."

The Oracle and I were hard put to contain our glee at this unexpected bit of good fortune. It was a Thursday. The spell had to be cast on a Friday. We would need things that could most likely be found in the kitchen—a bunch of bay leaves, some sprigs of verbena, and a beeswax candle—as well as hairs from the heads of both parties—difficult to obtain with the two of them at home, but easy enough to harvest when they were out of the house. "Go! Go!" I told Antonella. "Don't worry about Cico and me. We're fine."

Rendered momentarily wary by the enthusiasm with which I greeted her impending departure, Antonella peered at me suspiciously, eyes narrowed. Doubtless she was considering whether the fine cutlery would be there when she returned. Then she evidently thought better of it, for in the end she only shrugged and left.

As soon as we heard the back door shut behind her, I made my way down the hall to Cesare's room. It was the first time I had ventured out of the bedroom since I had arrived in Casteldurante a fortnight before, except to go out onto the balcony. Luckily, I had heard Cesare walk down the hall toward that room and open and shut its door often enough that I had a good idea where it was in relation to my own. It was larger than my room and airier still, but furnished in much the same luxurious manner, the principal difference being that it lacked a balcony and looked out on an inner courtyard rather than the piazza. But I had little time for exploration. I did not know how long Antonella would be or when I would have another such opportunity in the near future to obtain what was needed for the spell. I located an ivory-backed hairbrush on a dressing table, along with a fine linen handkerchief embroidered with the initials CB; I pulled a wad of hair from the brush and wrapped it securely in the handkerchief.

Then I made my way downstairs. Here I was in unfamiliar territory. However, it is never hard to locate the kitchen of a house and, once I had rifled through a few drawers and opened a few cabinet doors, I was able to find the requisite bay leaves, verbena sprigs, and beeswax candle.

From there it was a small matter of opening a door to discover the room just off the kitchen—Antonella's spare windowless bedroom, which resembled nothing so much as a nun's cell with its iron bedstead and lumpy mattress and the little wooden cross that hung above the narrow bed. A hairbrush—made of tortoiseshell this time—lay on the bedside table. I hastily removed a wad of hair from this brush as well and wrapped it in another handkerchief, this one of cambric and embroidered with the initials AA. Job done, I hastened upstairs, closing the door tightly behind me.

The following night, after the household had retired and we were alone in our darkened room, the Oracle and I recast the spell, using Antonella and Cesare's hair this time. I left it to the Oracle to pronounce the mysterious Etruscan words: "*Ca suthi nesl amcie titial can l restias cal ca rathsle aperuce n ca thui ceshu lusver etva capuvane caresi carathsle.*"

"Not even I know what it means," the Oracle confided. "But I've been told by some pretty highly placed deities who shall go unnamed that my Etruscan accent was more than passable…and that was back in the day when there was still some Etruscan being spoken in pockets around Latium and Umbria."

With that, I blew out the candle and waited to see what tomorrow might bring.

The following morning, Cesare Bacigalupo rose from his big mahogany bed and padded across the tile floor in his bare feet to the shuttered window overlooking the enclosed courtyard. Opening the louvers of one shutter, he peered out. *What sort of day is it likely to be?* he wondered. Shards of white light stabbed at his eyes and, despite the earliness of the hour, a blast of wilting heat assaulted him, as if the outdoors were an immense oven the door of which he had just opened. Retreating to the porcelain wash basin by the armoire, he vigorously scrubbed his hands, arms, neck, and face and patted them dry with a white linen towel. After this he struggled into his corset. Cesare was a vain man and although he would have been mortified to hear that my brothers called him fat, nevertheless, in his secret heart, he would have agreed with them. He donned a crisp white linen shirt, pulled on tight buckskin breeches and a pair of braces to hold them up, and, sitting on the edge of the bed, worked his feet into a handsome pair of fawn-colored top boots cobbled of butter-soft leather.

All this was very much as per usual for Cesare. He was, after all, something of a dandy, very particular about his clothes and general appearance. As for the day itself, it was, ostensibly, at least, a normal sort of day. He had got up. That was typical. He had dressed. Now he would have his breakfast. Later he would make his way down to Bacigalupo & Son, then back along the Via San Maria Maddalena, through the Largo Paolo Scirri to home where he would first take lunch, then a nap. This was what he did of a Saturday, what he had done, year in, year out for the last five years. He was a creature of habit, always doing the same thing at the same time, predictable and dull as a clock.

However, thanks to the nocturnal meddling of the Oracle and me, there was something different about the way the Prior felt that particular morning, something he couldn't quite put his finger on. Although he felt well enough rested, he had a memory of having woken numerous times during the night... and in something of a state each time—perspiring, his heart chugging away like a train engine pulling up-mountain. It seemed to him that he must have dreamed strange, sensuous dreams, but he could not remember so much as a fragment of one of them. Just an image, a face, and, oddly enough, not the face he had conjured up on each of the nights following his wife's death—that is to say, my face—but, remarkably, even shockingly, the face of his second cousin, of Antonella Aiello, his housekeeper.

Slipping on a camel-colored frock coat, he wandered downstairs. Normally his gait would be brisk, his manner officious, but that day Cesare felt distracted, muzzy, and strangely excited all at the same time. He was going to see her! Antonella! She was going to bring him breakfast, the way she did every day. Oh, but he was a lucky man to have breakfast brought to him by such a creature! So tall! So slender! How could he have thought her too tall, too thin? And with what bright eyes! He could hardly wait, and yet…. He paused by the door of the kitchen, suddenly overcome with shyness. "Cousin Antonella!" he called out, his voice quavering slightly. "I'm up!"

"Congratulations!" came the tart reply from deep within the bowels of the kitchen, her lair. He dared not peek in. She did not like it when he poked his nose into her kitchen. "You have the entire house to call your own," she would tell him. "May I, at least, call the scullery mine?"

"I'll take my breakfast in the garden," he said timidly. "If you would be so kind," he added.

Antonella grunted in response. Well, she was a woman of few words, after all. An admirable quality in a woman. One of many admirable qualities that Antonella possessed. Why had he failed to see them before? How had he not noticed how striking she was? When she was right under his eyes these past…what was it? Going on seven years. That was correct. It had been seven years since Antonella Aiello had been absorbed into the household, entering not through the front door, as might be expected given the fact that she was a relative, but ignominiously, through the back, for Cesare's mother had from the very beginning treated the orphaned only child of her cousin more like her servant than her ward. That had been a mistake, Cesare realized now, a grievous mistake that he must put right. No, from here on out, Antonella should have full honors. He must see to that.

He entered the enclosed garden around which the house, Roman style, was constructed and sat down at the little, tile-topped table where he took breakfast on fine mornings. An unkempt tangle of roses and bougainvillea flanked by narrow beds of French lavender and rosemary, the garden was not large, but pretty enough with its little terra-cotta pots of basil and tarragon and its statue of St. Francis and marble birdbath. He waited for Antonella, as a-buzz as a beehive, all tremulous anticipation.

Back in the kitchen Antonella roused herself to action. She had been sitting slumped at the kitchen's battered oak table, steeped in blackest melancholy. Now she hauled her lanky, stooped self to her feet, all the while muttering to herself something along the lines of, "Always eating! Night and day! Day and night. 'Cousin, Antonella! Please and thank you!'" She began slamming pots and pans around, deeply relishing the commotion, before chancing upon the proper pot to make coffee and banging it down on the stovetop.

Ten minutes later she shuffled through the open French door, carrying a tray on which was set a demitasse cup, a small pitcher of coffee, another of warmed milk, and, under a white damask napkin, a plate of *farfalle*—airy pastries shaped like butterflies and sprinkled with confectioner sugar. She exuded resentment.

For his part, Cesare surveyed his second cousin with glowing admiration. "Why, cousin! How radiant you are looking today!"

Antonella stared at him, deeply shocked. Then, deciding that he must be mocking her, she sniffed. "It is ungentlemanly of you to make fun of so unfortunate a person as myself!"

"No, I mean it," Cesare insisted. "I was not making fun of you. I was just…making an observation." He leaned over and patted the seat of the other chair. "Come, sit with me! Have a farfalle!"

"No, thank you," Antonella replied suspiciously. "There's a day-old hard bun in the kitchen that no one, not even the birds would eat. However, as it is a sin to waste food, I had planned to make it and a little coffee my humble breakfast."

"When there are these lovely pastries?"

"What has come over you today?" Antonella demanded and fled. Once safely back in the kitchen, she grabbed the stale bun she had supposedly earmarked for her breakfast and hurled it into the garbage.

Was he being kind, and if so, why? There must be a reason. People were never kind without a reason. He must want something from her. What could it be?

She opened the cupboard and removed from it two farfalle, fresh this morning. She had secreted them there before serving Cesare his breakfast. She set them on a plate, poured some coffee from the pot into a cup, and sat down at the table in front of the pastries, which she proceeded to tear into small pieces suitable for dunking.

Perhaps he wanted to sack her and put in her place that scruffy little peasant girl. He was certainly fond enough of her. Fond! She snorted. Her lowly bedroom—as plain as a nun's cell—might be just off the kitchen, but there was nothing in the least wrong with her hearing. Cesare's midnight visits to my door, his yowling and his scratching, had not gone unheard. In fact, Antonella had on several occasions stolen out of her room, through the kitchen, down the hall that bisected the house, and into the downstairs foyer to listen. To listen and, should it be required, to intervene. The whole situation disgusted her—a grown man hankering after such a young girl, and his recently deceased wife's sister to boot! But then Antonella saw her second cousin as pompous, self-absorbed, and just the least bit off, like a cheese that has crossed over from a perfect ripeness into something suspiciously tangy. She would put nothing past him.

"That's right," she said aloud through clenched teeth. "Dismiss me. On the other hand, you could always just shoot me down in the street like an old beast of burden past its usefulness. Put me out of my misery. People have been known to do that even to horses of which they were very fond. Or dogs. Dismiss me! And put in my place a peasant girl who won't know how to polish silver or wax furniture or take care of a house that doesn't have a dirt floor! Who won't know how to wind a clock or launder fine linens!"

There came a tentative knock at the kitchen door, then, "Cousin Antonella?"

Him!

"What?" she demanded.

"May I have a word?"

"What about?"

"There's something I want to tell you."

"Go away!"

"But—"

"Leave me alone!" she cried in a voice that sounded like a cat being strangled.

What on earth was going on?

Flummoxed by the obvious distress into which his small attentions had plunged his housekeeper and unsure what to make of it—or of his own wayward and chaotic emotions—Cesare left home for the majolica factory, feeling distinctly beside himself and wobbly as he struck out in an easterly direction across the piazza. Bacigalupo & Son was located just across the Old Bridge and beyond the city wall on the Via San Maria Maddalena.

The factory foreman oversaw the manufacturing side of the business while a manager handled the export end with the assistance of a clerk. Both men had worked for Cesare's father and were so efficient and reliable that there was nothing in the least for him to actually do at the factory. Nevertheless, believing that his job was to inspire a sense of awe among his employees and to remind them that he, like God in His Heaven, was observing their every move, Cesare had made a habit of spending several hours of every day, save Sunday, at the factory, getting in everyone's way and generally making a nuisance of himself.

This morning, however, Cesare stopped mid-piazza and reconsidered his options. He felt all at sixes and sevens, whatever that meant. He simply could not stop thinking about Antonella—of her sparkling eyes, like obsidian, of her swarthy skin and beak of a nose, of the plain, yet adorable way she wore her hair in a tight knot at the back of her stringy neck! Surely his manager and foreman could do without him for a few hours. He was certainly paying them enough! He needed to talk to somebody and who better to pour out his heart to than his old friend Pellicola?

Cesare turned around and headed off in the opposite direction, traversing the length of the Via Filippo Ugolini, past the convent of San Francesco and the little Cappella di Cola, across the bridge and through the old city gate to where the doctor's rambling stone house was located.

The Famiglia Pellicola came as close as Casteldurante got to old-fashioned landed gentry. Indeed, its original considerable holdings, along with the enviable title of Count, had been presented to the doctor's direct ancestor in the mid-fifteenth century by none other than the Duke of Urbino, Federico da Montefeltro, in payment for some sort of unspecified services rendered. Through the centuries since the Renaissance, much of the original estate had been sold off to pay debts, one parcel or vineyard at a time. The house, however, remained in the family, that is to say it remained in the possession of Dr. Pellicola, the last of his line, as did a large garden devoted to the cultivation of medicinal herbs and several acres of arable land, good for growing wheat and fennel, beets and cauliflower. A certain Farmer Palumbo worked these for Dr. Pellicola. The estate, diminished though it may have been, nevertheless generated sufficient income that Dr. Pellicola was able to live reasonably comfortably, provided he did not stray into undue extravagance.

Cesare knocked twice on the heavy wooden door, which was eventually opened by Isabella, Dr. Pellicola's housekeeper. Isabella had one arthritic hip and sciatica. As a consequence, she got nowhere fast. "Good morning, Signor Bacigalupo," she said, looking wary and disapproving. The doctor and

Cesare's relationship dated back to their childhood, to school days when they had been inseparable. Even then, the housekeeper had believed Cesare to be a bad influence on her young master. He was forever getting the doctor into trouble. To be sure, it was the doctor who always came up with the ideas. He was the clever one. However, Cesare was always there to egg him on, to enable him. More recently, Cesare had financially backed some of the doctor's more outlandish and dubious schemes. All of these involved dead animals—wolves and badgers, wild dogs and cats—brought to him by Farmer Palumbo or other neighborhood farmers and hunters, to whom Cesare paid a small fee. For Matteo Pellicola was a keen student of necropheia—the art of embalming. And because Cesare shared this interest (if not the doctor's strong stomach) and was much more affluent, it was the Prior who underwrote Pellicola's experiments. These consisted of the concoction of either embalming fluids, which were injected into the corpse, or soaking solutions, in which the corpse was suspended, and were made out of exotic and often expensive oils, unguents, and spirits or chemicals and compounds. To date, none of these experiments had proved successful; it would, after all, be another half a century before formaldehyde came into use.

"Good morning, Isabella," Cesare greeted the housekeeper. His manner was overly hearty. Isabella always made him feel like a seven-year-old caught doing something disgusting and despicable, and indeed, when he had been a seven-year-old (and an eight-year-old and a nine-year-old) that had often been the case. Taking his handkerchief from the breast pocket of his frock coat, he mopped his forehead. Even now, Isabella made him break out in a sweat.

The housekeeper glared at him, then crossed herself as though it was Satan himself come to call and said, "I expect you want to see the doctor. He's in the garden." Turning abruptly on her heel, she lurched down the corridor; Cesare trotted along behind her.

The Casa Pellicola predated the expansion of Casteldurante outside its medieval walls and was charmingly rustic in the haphazard way of country homes of the time, with stuccoed walls, low ceilings, wooden beams, and small arched windows equipped with heavy wooden shutters. No two rooms were on the same level so that climbing two or three steps was required every time one wanted to enter or exit a room—a situation that greatly aggravated Isabella's bad hip and contributed to her general state of misery. She led Cesare across the wide expanse of the main drawing room, down another flight of steps to a corridor that led past the kitchen, up three steps, through an arched door to the outside and out onto a terrace overlooking the doctor's extensive herb garden. It took up nearly an acre of land backing onto the swollen bend in the river known as the Gorga del Riscatto. It contained such useful herbs as angelica, goat's rue, orange hawkweed, elecampane, and monkshood—herbs from which could be fabricated medicaments to address all manner of ailments and some poisons besides. From the balcony Cesare could see that his friend was harvesting lavender; the basket he carried over his arm was full of purple spikes.

Isabella cupped her mouth with her hands and yelled, "Oh, Doctor! Signor Bacigalupo to see you!" Then, to Cesare's great relief, she abruptly turned on her heel and hobbled painfully back inside the house, letting the door slam behind her.

Doctor Pellicola shaded his eyes with his hands and peered up at the house. "Ah, Bacigalupo! It's you! Come down! Join me!"

Cesare descended the steps leading from the terrace to the garden and walked the short distance to where his friend stood. The two men shook hands. Cesare cast a backward glance at the house. "What am I to do? Your Isabella does not like me."

"Isabella has never liked you and never will. Why start worrying about it now?"

"But what have I ever done to offend her?"

"She disapproves of you. She thinks you are a bad influence on me. If I go to Hell, she will hold you personally responsible."

"Whereas, if I go to Hell, it will be a source of some rejoicing for my Antonella," said Cesare glumly. "Why should your housekeeper love you and mine despise me? Am I not as lovable as you?"

"Evidently not," the doctor replied. "But consider this. If I die, my cousin from Fermignano is heir to my estate…and, if you think Isabella doesn't approve of you, words cannot begin to describe how much she loathes poor Pepe. But what brings you to Casa Pellicola so early? I did not expect you until the afternoon. Not ill, I hope." It was Cesare's habit of a Saturday to drop by his friend's house sometime after siesta to smoke a fat cigar and drink a drop of grappa and check on the progress of various scientific experiments.

Cesare shook his head and sighed. "Not ill. Just in need of counsel."

"Well, you have come to the right place," said his friend,

"for I am, as usual, full of good advice! Please, sit down." He gestured to a stone bench and the two men sat side by side, looking out at the river. "What is on your mind, dear fellow?"

"I woke up this morning to some startling news," said Cesare. "Or, rather, I had a revelation." He shook his head woefully. "The truth is, I scarcely know where to begin."

"In the middle," counselled Pellicola. "Begin in the middle. You can always work your way back."

Cesare took a deep breath. "All right. Here goes. I woke up this morning to find that I have fallen in love..."

Pellicola rolled his eyes. He laid his hand on his friend's arm. "With Concetta's little sister. Are you just realizing that now?"

Cesare stared at him. "No. I mean. Yes, I *was* in love with her. Or infatuated. I can't imagine why. She is just a child and a scruffy one at that. I speak..." He hesitated.

Intrigued, the doctor leaned in closer. "You speak...for God's sake, man, spit it out!"

"I speak..." Cesare closed his eyes and whispered, "I speak of *Antonella!*"

The doctor was surprised. "Antonella? Surely you don't mean Antonella Aiello?"

Cesare nodded. He looked abashed.

"But how is that even possible? As you well know, I am not particularly partial to the ladies and, indeed, have no small difficulty telling them apart. However, even I recognize that Antonella is not the sort of woman one falls in love with."

"My head agrees with you, but my heart begs to differ," said Cesare. "Advise me, dear friend. What shall I do?"

Dr. Pellicola stroked his goatee, considering his response. He supposed Cesare must remarry. He had one son, it was true, but one could hardly count on children living to adulthood. The least little thing seemed to carry them off—a fever, a stomach ache—or else they might set themselves on fire or slice off their own head with a scythe. Frightfully accident-prone, children, which was why, he supposed, it was wise to have as many of them as possible if your heart was set upon having an heir. And Cesare's was. Pellicola knew that. For Bacigalupo & Son, there must be sons and there was just one way to get them.

That being the case, Pellicola reviewed Cesare's options with an eye to his own advantage. Were his friend to marry a townswoman of standing, she would inevitably exercise more control over his friend than would his former housekeeper. And if she didn't, her family would. In other words, were Cesare to marry a townswoman, he might not be allowed to "play" with Pellicola, as Isabella so tartly put it, to the same extent as he was now at liberty to do. The doctor shook his head. No, no. That would not do. Not at all.

Moreover, were Cesare to obtain a wife with expensive taste in, say, jewelry or hats or dresses from Milan and Paris, then his old chum might not be able to so generously fund the doctor's various experiments. That was definitely no good. While it was true that Antonella's status would rise were Cesare to wed her, it would probably only ever attain a point halfway between that of a servant and a wife, meaning that Antonella might be more easily managed than a higher status woman.

All things considered, it would better suit Pellicola's ends for Cesare to marry his housekeeper than someone of his own rank. Accordingly, he replied, "Why not?"

"You mean it?"

"I do."

"She comes from a good family, after all," Cesare grasped at straws. "She is my second cousin. And she was educated in a convent until she came to us. She has a smattering of Latin, I believe."

"Always useful."

"And French."

"What more do you need?"

"But what if she says no, Matteo? Because the way that she treats me...I sometimes think she doesn't much like me."

"Don't be absurd!" Pellicola laughed. "That is just her manner. Believe me, there is not a woman alive who would prefer being a housekeeper to being the lady of the house. Now, I'm not saying that some persuasion won't be required. Some blandishments, perhaps. Candy, flowers. That sort of thing. Perhaps one of Petrarch's sonnets. But, in the end, Antonella will say yes. Mark my words."

"All right," agreed Cesare, at once happy and wary. "It's decided then. I shall ask her today. For, in truth, I cannot bear to wait any longer." He cast a sideways glance at the basket resting on the doctor's knees. "What's the lavender for?"

"Oil of lavender. But what am I thinking of? Zounds!" Pellicola slapped himself lightly on the forehead with the heel of his hand. "I forgot to tell you about my new subject—or should I say, *our* new subject, for I assume you are footing the bill as usual."

Cesare was intrigued. "We have a new subject?"

"We do, and she's our first *primate!*" Pellicola grinned. It was a ghastly sight given his somewhat pointed teeth. "A chimpanzee, to be precise, by the name of Arabella."

Cesare was astonished. "What? A chimpanzee? And you didn't think to tell me this great news?" The two of them had been trying for some time to work out how they might obtain a human cadaver to work on. According to civil law, only the corpses of executed felons might be used in medical experiments and these were devilishly hard to come by. A chimpanzee, given its uncanny similarity to a human being, was surely the next best thing.

"I was going to tell you this afternoon," Pellicola responded. "She is the deceased pet of an Arabic merchant of my acquaintance who sold her to me. Quite cheaply, too, you'll be happy to know. He sent a man down with her early this morning. I was thinking of using a mixture of vermilion, turpentine, and oil of lavender. Hence the lavender. Have you time to look in?"

"Indeed, I do!" said Cesare, appalled and delighted at the same time. He had a notoriously weak stomach, particularly when it came to dead creatures. On the other hand, he could never resist a peek.

"You won't faint this time?" Pellicola asked.

"I can't promise that," Cesare told him. "However, I shall endeavor not to."

"Fair enough," replied the doctor, who kept a supply of smelling salts in the laboratory for the express purpose of reviving his friend and fellow conspirator. "Come along then."

That Saturday I had risen with the dawn, too agitated to sleep in. Had the spell once again worked its magic on Cesare? How would I know? When would it be confirmed? And how?

At about eight, there had been some commotion from downstairs—doors were slammed, angry words exchanged—but commotion, I knew, was not out of the ordinary where Antonella was involved. For a woman with little to say and none of it good, she made a great deal of noise.

Flora appeared three quarters of an hour later to collect Cico and bring me my breakfast; she was not happy to have been charged with the latter task. "As if I was a common servant! Bringing *you* breakfast! It's not in my contract, I tell you, and I won't be putting up with it! The Prior'll have to find another wet nurse for that little ingrate if *she* don't smarten up!"

"Why did she have you bring it?" I asked. "She's always brought it herself before."

"How should I know?" Flora fumed. "All high and mighty, she is, with her airs. She thinks that she's better than me. Wouldn't talk to the likes of me, she wouldn't. Too good for that. But you know what? I overheard her talking to herself in the kitchen like a crazy woman."

"What was she saying?" I asked eagerly.

Flora gave me a cool stare. "Do I look like the kind of person that listens in on other people's conversations with themselves?" she asked and left.

I think that particular Saturday was perhaps longest of

my very long life; certainly it seemed it. The Oracle and I waited and waited. We sat on the balcony until it became too warm and we had to go in. I wrote a long letter to my family. I listened as Sibylla told me for the third or fourth or fifth time, about something that happened to her a thousand years ago and that might have been funny then, but, clearly, you had to have been there.

Finally, after what seemed like an absolute eternity, Cesare returned for lunch. We heard the front door open, then shut behind him, the sound of voices and the slamming of what must have been the kitchen door. I waited impatiently for him to make an appearance, for he always paid a little visit to me just before lunch. Not that day, however. Finally, I could stand the suspense no longer. "I don't care," I told the Oracle. "I've got to see what's going on. I'm going downstairs." I hurriedly dressed in the clothes I had worn on my journey to Casteldurante—skirt, bodice, apron, and chemise—and wrangled my unruly hair into some semblance of order. I was ready for anything, but, most particularly, for getting out of that room. Despite all its elegance and comfort, I had come to detest it. And I had to find out whether the spell had worked.

"What about me?" Sibylla pleaded. She sounded forlorn.

"I'm sorry, Milady, but it would look very odd if I were to carry you downstairs with me. What would I say?"

"No odder than fetching me here from Montemonaco!" the Oracle protested.

"I'm sorry."

"But I'll miss everything!"

"Who knows if there will be anything *to* miss?"

"You will see how he looks at her," countered the Oracle. "You'll hear how he talks to her. You'll be able to *tell*."

"I'll give you a full report," I promised, growing more impatient with each minute that passed. I wanted to leave. I wanted to go downstairs. I wanted to get out.

"But it's not the same as being there!" she wailed.

I descended the stairs to the foyer for only the second time ever and arrived at a large, dark parlor crammed with uncomfortable looking furniture where I found Cesare awkwardly perched on the arm of a tub chair, lost in thought.

"Brother-in-law?" I ventured.

"Hallo! What?" He sounded startled. He stood, blinking at me as if he did not quite recognize me. Then, "Why... Maria, isn't it? I didn't expect to see you down here. What in Heaven's name are you doing up?"

So he'd forgotten my name, had he? That was a good sign. "It's Mariuccia," I replied, "and I'm feeling much better. Cico is down for his nap, so I thought I might get dressed and have lunch with you for a change."

He looked stricken.

"Is that all right?" I asked.

"Why, of course it is!" he said uncertainly. "But we shall have to tell Antonella. Wait a moment." He rubbed his hands together, hunching his shoulders as if there were a chill in the air. Then he retreated into an adjacent dining room. I heard him knock tentatively on a door. "Antonella?"

"What?"

"Our guest...what's her name...will be having lunch downstairs with me today. Is that all right?"

Silence.

"Antonella?"

"*Fine!*" came the reply.

"You don't sound like it's fine."

"It's *fine*, I tell you! Now, leave me alone!"

Next the sound of a lid clanging roughly down onto a pot...then of a dish hurled against the wall and shattering.

Cesare returned to the parlor, red-faced and perspiring. He mopped his face with a handkerchief. "You must forgive the poor dear. She doesn't like surprises."

"What surprise? It just means that she doesn't have to carry my lunch upstairs—"

Cesare cut me off. "Any surprise, any change whatsoever. Hers is a very delicate sensibility—exquisitely so. The least little thing sets her off. We must make allowances." He ushered me through to the dining room. Unlike the gloomy parlor, it was filled with light and simply furnished with a long table, half a dozen chairs, and a sideboard. He took his place at the head of the table, unfolded his napkin, and said, "Sit. Please. Anywhere."

After a moment's hesitation, I walked down to the opposite end of the table and sat down, facing him.

"So you're feeling better?" he asked.

"Much better. A little weak is all."

"And you didn't feel at all wobbly...coming downstairs?"

"No."

Conversation in this halting vein continued for perhaps a

quarter of an hour, made increasingly more awkward by the obvious fact that his mind was clearly elsewhere. He squirmed and fidgeted like a boy with fleas, yanking at his cravat and glancing surreptitiously in the direction of the door that led to the kitchen.

Finally, I announced, "I'm feeling a bit light-headed. I think I need to eat."

"Ah, yes, well," said Cesare. "You need to eat. We both need to eat. I wonder what's keeping the dear girl. She seems to be running a bit late. Perhaps I should just check."

The dear girl! I ducked my head so that he wouldn't see me smile. Yes! The spell had worked! He had clearly forgotten all about me; his attentions were now focused on his housekeeper.

Cesare rose and crossed over to the door. He knocked tentatively. "Oh, Antonella?"

"*What?*" A strangled sound from inside the kitchen.

"May I come in?"

"*No!*"

Silence.

"Antonella?"

"What do you want?"

"Just wondering how lunch is progressing."

"I'm making it as fast as I can. I only found out fifteen minutes ago that there would be *a guest!*"

"No rush," Cesare attempted to soothe her. "Just take your time." He returned to the table and sat down. "Poor darling. She's very excitable. Like a lovely filly, full of fire!"

I leaned in, gleeful. "What is Antonella's story anyway? I don't believe I know it."

Cesare brightened, delighted to be afforded the opportunity to talk about his housekeeper. "She is the daughter of my mother's cousin, who married, I fear, a rascal. In time, the scoundrel absconded and my mother's poor cousin subsequently died in childbed. Poor Antonella." He sighed. "My mother was the only mother she knew."

Poor Antonella, indeed, judging from what I had heard about the Dowager Bacigalupo.

"Antonella is quite accomplished," he continued proudly. "She attended a school for girls at the convent of San Franceso and can do all manner of needlework. She can read and write and do numbers; she even has a little Latin and French. And her penmanship!" He sighed rapturously. "Breathtaking!"

"Penmanship is so important," I said.

"It is!" said Cesare. He lowered his voice and leaned forward. "She had a vocation to become a Poor Clare, but the Mother Superior advised against it. She told my mother that Antonella was too cross to be a nun. Can you imagine? Too cross! When she has such a lovely disposition! I think the Mother Superior mistook high spirits for irritability! Well, the Poor Clares' loss is our gain!"

The door to the kitchen swung open and Antonella appeared, bearing a soup tureen. We turned to look at her.

She bristled. "Why are you looking at me like that?"

"Who? Us?"

"Whatever do you mean?" This from Cesare.

"Like cats look at a mouse!"

"Nonsense, dearest," said Cesare. "We are only hungry for our lunch. Though I must say, you are looking particularly charming today. I have always admired how you carry off that *fichu*."

Antonella stared at him, incredulous.

"Come along! Come along, cousin," Cesare cajoled her. "Let's eat. I can hardly wait to sample what delicacy you have prepared for us."

"It's tortellini in broth," Antonella said flatly. "Just ordinary old tortellini in broth. You've never much liked it."

"Not liked it? When it's my absolute favorite? And how not, when it has been so lovingly prepared by such delicate hands?"

Antonella's mouth fell open, then snapped shut. She walked over to the table, put down the tureen in front of me—roughly—and, without a word, turned on her heel and returned to the kitchen. The door slammed behind her.

"You must forgive her," Cesare said in a low voice. "She's very shy."

"Is there any bread?" I asked.

"Oh, Antonella!" Cesare called. "Bread?"

A hand protruded from the kitchen door holding a basket of buns.

Cesare started to rise.

"Please!" I leapt to my feet. "Let me." I crossed over to the door and took the basket from the hand. The hand withdrew; the door closed.

I served up the soup. It was very flat-tasting. "The tortellini could use some nutmeg. And the broth needs more salt."

"I'm in the next room!" This from the kitchen. "I can hear every word you say."

"Oh, now you've hurt her feelings!" Cesare exclaimed softly.

"Sorry!" I mouthed.

We finished our soup in silence.

"If you'll excuse me," Cesare told me. "I'm going to try to talk with her. Smooth her ruffled feathers, so to speak."

"Of course," I said. Then, growing bolder, I said, "This afternoon when Cico's with Flora, I thought I'd go out for a bit of a stroll. Do some exploring. I've seen nothing of Casteldurante except what I can see from the balcony." I braced myself, expecting him to protest or even to forbid me from striking out on my own, a young unchaperoned woman in a strange city. What would people think? What if something untoward were to befall me? To my surprise, however, he seemed to barely register my plan, so preoccupied was he with the state of Antonella's wounded feelings.

"Yes, well, good idea," he said distractedly. "Fresh air and all that." He was staring at the kitchen door as if it were a formidable palisade he must assail.

Triumphant, I excused myself.

"Antonella! Oh, Antonella!" I heard as I ascended the stairs to my room. "Please, dear cousin! Let me in!"

That afternoon I ventured out into Casteldurante for the first time. It might have been a small city when compared to the likes of Rome or Milan—at that time the old city walls held perhaps a thousand households within their embrace, while another thousand lay without—but to a country girl like me, it seemed both vast and impossibly sophisticated. I was entranced by the Metauro, that lazy, insolent river, thick as treacle and grass-green in hue. Its leisurely meanderings give the town its contorted shape and make of its streets baffling rabbits' warrens. I was astounded by the height of its sand-colored buildings—often several stories high, a thing unheard of in Montemonaco where the closest thing to a second floor was a loft. And the smells and the sounds! Not to mention the people—so many of them coming and going. It was breathtaking.

I made a mental note of the rectory where Pasquale lived with his parents and doddering old Padre Eusebio—a modest two story house with green shutters, separated from Casa Bacigalupo by the little chapel of Capella Cola—and ventured briefly into the dark little church itself, which I understood from Cesare to be funded by the Confraternity he served as Prior. It paled, however, when compared to the city's imposing Duomo, which I also visited.

When I returned home for the evening, just as Vespers were being rung—a virtual cacophony of bells—I felt both exhausted and exhilarated. Satisfied that the spell had worked and, in any case, not wishing to repeat the awkward ordeal that had been my lunch with Cesare, I told Antonella that I would take a light supper in my bedroom, collected Cico from Flora, and retired for the night.

I was still telling the Oracle about all the places I had seen, when there came a sharp knock on my door. We fell abruptly silent, then I cleared my throat and called out, "Come in!"

Antonella opened the door. She was carrying a tray

with my supper on it—a small basket of bread and a bowl of gnocchi in a bechamel sauce. "Talking to yourself again? That's what crazy people do."

"I was telling Cico of my adventures,"

"Might as well tell a post or a donkey for all he understands!"

"That's how babies learn to talk. By listening. Everyone knows that."

I relieved her of the tray and was turning back toward the small table where I took my meals, when Antonella cleared her throat. "I was wondering. Might I have a word with you? I don't know who else to talk to."

I hesitated, but then said, "Well, of course." I set the tray down and turned to face her. "If you want."

"It's just that…have you noticed that my cousin has been acting…I don't know… weirdly?" She looked very awkward, standing there in the door, wringing her hands and shifting her weight from one foot to the other.

I smiled. "Only that he appears very fond of a certain young lady."

Antonella blushed. I had never seen her blush before; it made her look like an eggplant. "He…he just asked me to marry him." She had difficulty forcing the words out, as if she could not quite believe what she herself was saying.

I shrugged. "I suppose I should be upset seeing my sister so rapidly replaced by another. But, you know. Life goes on."

"So you think he's…serious?" Antonella asked.

"Why not?"

"Because the way he's acting…it's like the way he was acting toward you earlier."

"Better you than me!"

"But why? I don't understand. Why the sudden change?" She slumped despondently against the door lintel, which looked not in the least comfortable.

"Why not? You are a woman. He is a man. I personally don't get it, but it seems to be the way things work. If you don't mind, I'm going to start eating. I don't want my dinner to get cold."

"Go ahead," Antonella replied glumly. I sat down and unfolded my napkin. "He insisted I eat dinner with him," she said. "It was hellish. I kept telling him that if his mother knew I was sitting there with him at the table, she would be turning in her grave. She never allowed me to sit at table with them. Never. And he said he didn't care what his mother thought; she was dead. And I said, maybe dead to you. And he said never mind her and tried to give me the ring, the one he gave Concetta, his mother's ring. Right then and there he got down on his knee and tried to squeeze that ring on my finger."

"Yes, and…"

Antonella let out a kind of anguished yelp. "I ran out of the room and locked myself in the kitchen."

"I don't know what the fuss is all about. It's a very handsome ring."

"Don't you understand? It's her ring—*hers!* No sooner had it touched my flesh than it burned me! A ring of fire!"

"Don't be such a ninny!" This from the Oracle.

I froze, my fork in midair, my mouth half open.

Antonella stiffened. She clutched her throat and glanced wildly about the room. "Who's there?"

"Who do you think, you useless chit?" asked Sibylla. "It is I, Lucrezia Bacigalupo, your cousin and tormenter!"

I ducked my head and pretended to cough into my napkin.

"You see?" cried Antonella, distraught. "I told you this room was haunted!"

"I didn't dispute that it was haunted," I pointed out. "Just that you let that put you off."

"How can that not put you off? A ghost who's forever telling you you're stupid and ugly and not worth the food you eat?"

"Ghosts are always cranky. They are neither here nor there and such ambivalence irritates them no end. My nonna was as mild as a day in May when she was alive, but she made a most unpleasant ghost."

But the Oracle was not done with the housekeeper. "I hear that you've sunk your claws into my poor son's heart! That he has given you my ring. Will you marry him for his money and station and play him for a fool?"

"I want nothing to do with your stupid son or your ring!" Antonella stamped her foot. "It's him who's after me!"

"I doubt that!" the Oracle mocked her. "What man in his right mind would want you for a bride?"

"Your stupid son, that's who!"

"If he is, then he has been bewitched. Have you bewitched him, vixen? Are you a witch?"

Sibylla was skating a little too close to the truth here for my comfort. "Uh—" I began, but Antonella overrode us both.

"I haven't bewitched him and I'm not a witch! *You're* the witch!"

"No, you're the witch!"

"No, you!" Antonella was furious now, red-faced and shaking with rage. "You're just angry because I poisoned you and you didn't see it coming. Did you? Did you? Not until it was too late! Not until you were dying!"

A split second later, realizing that she had actually spoken these words aloud and in the presence of another human being, Antonella clamped her mouth shut. She looked at me, eyes widening with terror. I stared back, rendered temporarily speechless by her confession. Then the housekeeper twisted to her right, her left arm coming up alongside her head as if to shield it. She dropped to one knee, where she cowered, trembling. "Addio!" she sobbed. "Addio! I am ruined!"

I hesitated for a moment, then put down my fork and laid down my napkin. I stood awkwardly and made my way over to the housekeeper, placed a hand on her heaving shoulder and said, "Don't worry, Antonella. I won't reveal your secret...on one condition."

The housekeeper looked up at me, her eyes swollen, her face tear-streaked. "Condition?"

"That you accept my brother-in-law's generous proposal."

That night, shortly before midnight, I was awakened by a loud creaking and rending noise, accompanied by the high-pitched whine of glass under stress. Moments later came the sound of an explosion, followed by a crash. I sat bolt upright in bed, my heart pounding. "What in Heaven's name?"

"Oh, not to worry!" The Oracle sounded gleeful. "Just a little something I cooked up."

"Cooked up?" I demanded. "What do you mean 'cooked up?'"

"Oh, just a wee thing called an earth tremor."

"You caused an earth tremor?"

"Who else? The fairies? Those silly dwarves? And if my aim was true, that little chapel your brother-in-law is so fond of is in ruins right about now."

"The Capella Cola?"

"The same!"

Cico emitted a thin wail.

"Look what you've done!" I cried with exasperation. "You've woken Cico! And Flora's not in until tomorrow morning. I'm going to have a devil of a time trying to get him back to sleep now!" I stumbled out of bed and made my way over to his bassinet. Just as I was picking him up, I heard Cesare's door open and his footsteps in the hall. A moment later and he was rapping on our door. "Is my son all right?" He paused only long enough to hear my reply before noisily descending the stairs, two at a time, calling out, "Antonella! Antonella, my dove! Are you injured?"

This was followed a moment later by the sound of scuffling. "What? What are you doing?" Antonella screeched. "Leave me alone! Have you no decency?"

Holding Cico, I opened the door and stepped out into the hall. Cesare was trudging back up the stairs. "Where are you going?" I asked. "Don't you want to see what made that terrible noise?"

He shook his head, despondent. "Whatever the damage was, it will be there in the morning and that will come soon enough."

"Not for me!" I said. "I want to see what happened."

"Suit yourself," he said glumly. "I'm going to bed."

As soon as we heard the door to his bedroom shut behind him, the Oracle cried, "Well, what are we waiting for? I want to see my handiwork! It's been quite a few hundred years since I've wrecked anything. I want to see if I still have the touch!"

A quarter of an hour later, I joined Pasquale, his parents, and Padre Eusebio—all of us in our night clothes—in the ruined chapel. The damage was extensive, though by no means complete, much to the chagrin of Sibylla, whose jug I carried in a bag slung over my shoulder. The tremor had caused the wall directly behind the Cappella di Cola's altar to crumble into limestone dust and collapse into the chancel, burying the ancient altar. Spikes of brightly stained glass peppered the pile of stone and debris. And where the upper wall of the clerestory had loomed there now stretched an expanse of night sky, black as soot and pocked with bright stars. Not utter devastation, but impressive nonetheless.

I was for once unencumbered, having resolved at the last moment to leave Cico in Antonella's charge. I was beginning to realize that knowing the housekeeper's dreadful secret gave me considerably more leverage over her than I had had previously.

"*Ker-choo!*" sneezed the priest. A cloud of limestone dust hung in the air; more dust mantled every surface in the ruined church. "*Ker-ker-choo!*" He peered at me, squinting and frowning. "You look familiar. Aren't you the little girl who put mugwort up my nose?"

"I am."

"What was your name again? Maria? Marianna? No. Marina!"

"Mariuccia."

"That's right. Mariuccia Umbellino. Why are you here, Mariuccia Umbellino, and not there in those terrible mountains full of witches?"

"She is staying with the Prior, Padre," said the sacristan. "I told you and so did the Prior. You remember. The Prior married the family's eldest daughter."

"Yes, yes, of course!" said the priest. "Slipped my mind. My mind is very slippery these days. Practically nothing sticks. So, what do you think? Is God moving in mysterious ways? Should we be reading anything into this calamity? Is it a sign? Or...oh, but...but...wait! Perhaps this is the Witch of Monte Vettore's doing! Mariuccia Umbellino, did your mother not warn us that the Old One would take revenge upon her persecutors?"

Much to my relief, given that this was indeed what had happened, Pio put an end to this line of inquiry. "Now, Padre, you know that this was bound to happen one of these days, given the sorry state of the foundation. It's time to fill in the crypt."

"What's a crypt?" I asked.

173

"Burial vaults located under the church," said Pio. "In the old days, parishioners were laid to rest there. Then the Edict of St. Cloud was proclaimed, requiring corpses to be buried outside city walls. My father before me—also this chapel's sacristan—had to remove all the bodies from the crypt and rebury them in the San Vivaldo cemetery in order to comply with the law. This left a large crawl space beneath the church that was not reinforced by beams or posts or any other structural elements—highly unstable. That's what accounts for the buckling you see and the uneven floor."

"Enough of that kind of talk!" said Padre Eusebio. "I won't hear of it! While there's breath in this old body, every tile in this floor is going to remain exactly where it is!" Turning on his heel, he stomped off in the direction of the sacristy. A moment later there was the sound of the door that led from the sacristy to the outdoors opening and closing.

"What's with him and this floor?" Pasquale asked. "Every time you mention reinforcing the foundation, he has a fit."

Pio sighed. "You tell me. I'll fetch the Prior first thing in the morning. He can decide what's to be done. We should all get some sleep. Tomorrow will be a busy day. Pasquale will light you to your door, Signorina Umbellino."

With that, we went our separate ways, Pio and his wife in the direction in which Padre Eusebio had exited and Pasquale and I through the door that led from the church to the piazza. Pasquale held the lantern aloft so that I could pick my way safely through the rubble and escorted me all the way to the front door of the Casa Bacigalupo where he wished me goodnight.

"Mark my words. That boy has eyes for you," the Oracle advised me once we were safely inside.

"Well, I don't have eyes for him," I replied. And I didn't.

As the bells in the campanile tolled nine the following morning, I deposited Cico with Flora, fended off the Oracle's pleas to, once again, be borne along with me, and headed next door to see the damaged chancel in the daylight. It was already a bustling scene. People milled around in the piazza, poking their heads in for a gawk, while Cesare presided over the work, looking pompous and self-important. He was joined by Dr. Pellicola and another, rather fantastical looking individual—small and wiry, with a wooden peg leg about an inch shorter than his remaining limb, a discrepancy that caused him to list to one side when he stood and to lurch when he walked. The three men looked on as Pasquale and another boy named Giorgio loaded rubble into wheelbarrows.

I made my way over to Pasquale's mother, who was sweeping shards of stained glass into a pile. "What's going on?" I asked.

"Once the rubble is removed, they're going to lift up the tiles and pour sand into the vaults," Signora Assaroti explained.

"But what about Padre Eusebio? Won't he be angry?"

She shrugged. "Yes, but I let him sleep in this morning. By the time he realizes what's happened, it will be too late."

"Who is that man with Cesare and Dr. Pellicola?" I asked.

Signora Assaroti snorted. "That's Dr. Pellicola's appalling cousin from Fermignano. Giuseppe Passalacqua is his name—Pepe for short. He went to Egypt with Napoleon twenty years ago and has only just returned. It is rumored he was fleeing French authorities who sought to imprison him in Château d'If for the crime of selling Egyptian antiquities he didn't own. At his best he is a most terrible ne'er do well, a slackard perpetually at loose ends; at his worst, a thief and a blackguard."

I wandered over to where Cesare and his companions were standing.

"The little patient!" Dr. Pellicola greeted me. "Good to see you up and about, Signorina Umbellino! Feeling a bit better, I take it?"

"Much better, thank you."

"Allow me to introduce you to my dear cousin, Giuseppe Passalacqua, who is staying with me for a while. Pepe, this is Bacigalupo's little sister-in-law. She has been very ill of an ague, but now, as you may discern from the roses abloom in her cheeks, her health has improved considerably."

Pepe smiled down at me. It was a ghastly smile. His haggard face was tanned to leather by the Egyptian sun and a livid scar bisected his right cheek. "Charmed, I am sure," he said.

Embarrassed by the attention and not knowing what else to do, I muttered something vague.

"This work would go much faster if we had more than just the two wheelbarrows," Cesare observed. "Unfortunately, these were all my foreman could spare today."

"Too bad this didn't happen in Fermignano!" Pellicola said to his cousin. "If it had, there'd be no lacking for wheelbarrows!"

The two men laughed. "You've got that right!" said Pepe. "In Fermignano, every family has its own wheelbarrow. What's more, they are most beautifully painted. Indeed, some you might call works of art!"

"Painted wheelbarrows?" asked Cesare. "Really? But what do the Fermignani use these decorative wheelbarrows for?"

"For the famous Palio della Rana, of course! The Frog Race! Don't tell me you haven't heard of the Frog Race?"

"I have not!"

"Then I am astonished at your ignorance! The Palio della Rana is nothing less than my town's signature event! It is a celebration of the greatest magnitude and solemnity, held on the first Sunday after Easter and preceded by a magnificent procession in historic costume."

Cesare shook his head. "I'm sorry. Never heard of it."

"What about you, Signorina?" Pepe turned to me. "Don't tell me that you too, have never heard of the Palio della Rana?"

I shook my head. "I'm sorry. No."

"It is an extremely odd festivity," said Dr. Pellicola, "and a mysterious one. No one knows its origin, which dates back to pre-Roman times. Pepe, you tell."

"Each of Fermignano's seven districts is represented by a wheelbarrow in which there sits a frog," Pepe explained. "A district champion is selected whose job it is to push the wheelbarrow. There is a course laid out and whoever reaches the finish line first with his frog still in the wheelbarrow wins. The challenge, of course, is to keep the frog from jumping out of the wheelbarrow. You would not believe how difficult that is."

"If memory serves, you won the Palio one year, did you not?" the doctor asked.

Pepe shrugged. "In a manner of speaking. Unfortunately, I was disqualified. As soon became clear, my frog had expired en route. Beatrice was its name. After my fiancée."

"It died as a result of breathing the glue fumes," the doctor explained. "Am I remembering that correctly, Pepe?"

"You are, cousin, for you see, I had glued its back to the inside of the wheelbarrow."

"Can you believe that, in the hundreds and hundreds of years that the Palio della Rana has been taking place, no one has thought to glue the frog to the inside of the vehicle?" the doctor marveled. "Either you are extremely clever, cousin, or your fellow townspeople are not very inventive."

"Unfortunately, there was a great outcry over the incident, and I was plunged into considerable disrepute," Pepe said glumly. "My fiancée's father was so mortified that he broke off our engagement. Indeed, the Palio della Rana is the reason I left Fermignano altogether and sailed to Egypt with Napoleon."

"It was during the Egyptian campaign that poor Pepe lost his leg," the doctor told me.

"A camel fell on top of me," Pepe explained.

"Does this sort of thing often happen in Egypt?" the Prior asked. "Camels falling on people?"

Pepe shook his head. "Very seldom. Of course, the Egyptians were firing on us at the time and aren't terribly good shots. Do you have any idea how much a camel weighs?"

"A good deal, I should think!"

"Indeed, it does! Fortunately, I was able to salvage the leg itself. I take it with me wherever I go in a large carboy filled with whiskey."

"It is most remarkably preserved," the doctor interjected.

"Just a touch green," Pepe said modestly. "By the time it was amputated, a bit of gangrene had set in. Just a bit."

"The ladies tend to find it distressing, but you, Bacigalupo! You would enjoy it immensely."

"What about me?" I asked. "Can I see it?"

"Alas, Signorina," the doctor said. "I fear the sight of it might cause you to faint. For it is both terrible and wonderful to behold."

"Not me. I'm as brave as any boy and a leg in a jar—that's something you don't see every day!"

But wonders, as it fell out, were far from ceasing, for the next moment we heard the loud clatter of a shovel thrown to the tile floor and a strangled cry from Giorgio. "*Santo Iddio!* What horror is this?" Everyone turned to look toward the front of the chapel and the boys with the wheelbarrows.

"What is it?" Pio called out.

"I cannot say," replied Giorgio. "Just that it is the most terrible thing I have ever laid eyes upon!"

Pasquale laid down his shovel and came over to where his comrade stood. He took one look at whatever it was that Georgio had uncovered and staggered back a step, saying "Ooof!" as though someone had just punched him in the stomach.

"Let me see!" Pio pushed the two boys aside to have a look. Then he cried out, "Prior! Doctor! Come! This you have to see!"

Cesare and the doctor hurried down the center aisle of the nave to the chancel, followed by me and, at a short distance, Pepe, whose peg leg made a thumping noise against the floor tiles as he hobbled behind.

To the right of the altar and behind it lay what appeared to be a shallow vault. In it was deposited the strangest creature that I, at any rate, had ever seen—the body (not the skeleton, but the *body*) of what must have been a very tall person, composed entirely of a bleached, but somehow leathery substance. Its head was turned to the right and inclined downward. Its mouth was stretched open in an expression of anguish, its eye sockets yawned large and empty, as did the oval aperture where the cartilage that had formed the creature's nose had once held sway. A dusty mop of matted hair still clung in patches to its head and scraps of clothing to its torso and limbs. Its fingernails were intact, long and curled like talons.

"Good heavens!" Cesare managed.

"My word!" Pellicola placed his monocle in his right eye and inclined closer for a better look.

Signora Assaroti laid down her broom and came forward. She peered at the creature. "All the angels and saints!" She crossed herself.

"You do know what it is, don't you?" asked Pepe.

Mute with astonishment, Cesare shook his head.

"If I've seen one, I've seen a hundred," Pepe boasted. "Well, I did spend the last twenty years in Egypt after all. It's a mummy, of course."

"You don't say!" the doctor exclaimed. "But how wonderful!"

"A mummy!" breathed Cesare. "A real mummy!"

"But how did he come to be buried in this place, thus preserved?" the doctor asked. "Why here and not the cemetery?"

"Perhaps Padre Eusebio would know."

"I'll wager he does!" said Signora Assaroti. "I'll wager he's known it all along and that's why he didn't want Pio to dig up the floor all these years!" With that, she started off in the direction of the sacristy.

"Where are you going?" cried her husband.

"To fetch that old coot!"

"But he's asleep!"

"He won't be when I wake him up!"

"*Caterina!*"

But she was gone.

"Confound it!" said Pio. "I was going to ask her to fetch some water. This is thirsty work."

"I'll get it for you!" I volunteered and started off after Signora Assaroti, exiting the sacristy by a side door and walking next door to the rectory. I knocked on the kitchen door several times and said, quite loudly, "Signora Assaroti, it's me, Mariuccia Umbellino, come to fetch water! Signora Assaroti!"

No response.

I slipped into the kitchen and peered about. Caterina was not there, but I could hear the sound of her pounding on a door on the same floor, crying, "Wake up, Padre! Wake up! Prior wants you. It's nearly ten o'clock in the morning, Father! Time for you to wake up!"

"Who? What? Prior? Prior who?" came Eusebio's thin bleat. "There have been so many Priors!"

"Prior Bacigalupo and Dr. Pellicola. They're in the chapel. They want to speak with you."

"They are young and I am old. Let them come here if they want to speak with me!"

"I'm coming in!"

"No! No! Don't come in! Caterina!"

The sounds of a scuffle ensued, followed by Signora Assaroti's exasperated, "Don't give me any trouble now, Padre. On with that cassock. No, never mind. I'll button it. Stop that! No, you're not going back to bed! Don't you dare!"

A few moments later, she appeared in the doorway with a disheveled Padre Eusebio in tow. "*Ooch! Ooch!*" he complained. "Where is the big toe of St. Alphonsus when you need it? Wait a minute! Mariuccia Umbellino! What are you doing here? Are you everywhere now?"

"They sent me for water. I knocked, but no one answered."

"There's a jug over there on the cupboard." Signora Assaroti pointed. "I filled it this morning. Come along, Padre. The Prior is waiting."

"Well, let him wait. What could be so important that he has to drag an old man out of bed?"

"Well, for one, a mummy has been discovered under the floor of the chancel!"

Eusebio stared at her, blinking. "What did you say?"

"I said, they've found a mummy under the floor of the chancel."

"They? Who are 'they'?"

"Pasquale and another boy."

"And they're digging up the floor? I told you not to dig up the floor!"

"It's too late, Padre! The floor is dug up and the cat is out of the bag!"

"What? Is there a cat under the floor? In a bag?"

"Not an actual cat in a bag." Signora Assaroti sounded exasperated. "A mummy!"

"A *mummy?*" Padre Eusebio pinched the loose folds of his forehead with his thumb and middle finger and squeezed his eyes closed. "Oh dear, oh dear!"

"What is it, Father? What's the matter?"

"That this should have happened…I thought for sure…"

"That *what* should have happened?"

"I feel ill," the priest muttered, looking vaguely around and patting his pockets haphazardly as though for something that he had lost—keys or some small object. "Please, Caterina, I must sit down."

"What's wrong, Father?"

"Dizzy," the priest all but whispered. "Heart palpitations." He lowered himself in jerky increments onto a chair.

"You're shivering, Father!" Taking off her shawl, Signora Assaroti draped it over the old man's shoulders.

As she did, the priest reached up and seized hold of her wrist with his bony fingers. "I don't want to talk to them, Caterina! I can't talk to them! You mustn't make me!"

"I don't understand. What are you afraid of?"

"Nothing! I'm afraid of nothing."

Pio appeared in the doorway. "What's taking so long? The Prior and the doctor want to get going." He glanced at me. "And I thought you were fetching us some water!"

"Sorry!" I jerked to sudden life, retrieving the jug from the cupboard.

"You talk to him," Signora Assaroti told her husband. "He's being impossible."

"Come on, Padre," said Pio. "There's a body buried under the floor. Do you know anything about that?"

"Nothing! I know nothing. Maybe it wandered in off the street, lifted the floor tiles and buried itself!"

"Now, Father!"

"Now, Father, what?"

"Now, Father, you're not telling the truth!"

"How do you know?"

"Because you are not looking me in the eye," Pio told him sternly. "And you're twitching."

"Tell them this. When my predecessor, Old Father... what's his name?"

"Father Basil?" Signora Assaroti supplied the name.

"When Father *Basil* ran out of room in the crypt, he buried a number of bodies under the altar. What an idiot he was! No sooner had he done that than the magistrate informed him he was not in compliance with health regulations. So he had to move all those bodies to San Vivaldo. There were two, maybe three of them. I don't know. Maybe more. Tell the Prior and *Il Dottore* that the fellow there must have been one Father Basil missed. The old man was practically blind! He could easily have missed a body. Or perhaps the doddering old fool forgot he was there. Most days he couldn't remember his own name. Tell them I know nothing about it." He stood. "That's it. That's all you're going to get from me. I'm going back to bed and if either of you try to stop me, I'll have a fit of apoplexy and die and it will be all your fault!"

He stripped Signora Assaroti's shawl from his shoulders

and flung it at her before hobbling defiantly off toward his bedroom. A moment later, we heard a loud creaking sound that signaled his return to bed.

"He's hiding something," Signora Assaroti said.

"I know," Pio replied.

"What could it be?"

Pio shrugged. "Who knows?"

"Well, no point in trying to get him to talk now. His guard is up."

"I suppose." Suddenly Pio remembered that I was still there. "Signorina Umbellino, please!"

"Sorry!" I said and fled with the water jug.

"What did Padre Eusebio have to say about our friend here?" Cesare asked. In my absence, Pasquale and Giorgio had managed to load the mummy onto a stretcher and were standing ready to convey it to Dr. Pellicola's laboratory.

Pio shrugged. "He says that Padre Basil must have missed this body when they made the transfer to San Vivaldo. Or perhaps he simply forgot about him. My own father served as his sacristan. When I was a boy, my mother used to send me out to look for the old man when he had wandered off. He'd get lost or tangled up in bramble bushes. By the end of his life, he was as guileless as a newborn baby."

"Whatever the reason for this happiest of oversights, I rejoice in my good fortune," said Pellicola. "I've wanted to get my hands on a mummy for as long as I can remember."

"It's true," Cesare said. "I've known him since boyhood, and he has always been fascinated by mummies."

"Ready, boys?" the doctor asked Giorgio and Pasquale. To Pio he added, "I'll send them back as soon as we've got this fellow safely ensconced in my laboratory."

Pepe tugged at his sleeve. "They'll want to see my leg while they're there, don't you think?"

"Oh, yes!" said Pasquale and Giorgio, word of the leg suspended in whiskey clearly having preceded Pepe's arrival in Casteldurante.

"May I come?" I asked. "I'd like to see your leg too."

"Mariuccia!" cried Signora Assaroti. "Why would you want to see such a dreadful thing as a severed limb floating in a jar? Surely such a sight would frighten you and give you bad dreams."

"Not me," I assured her. "I'm very brave."

"That's settled then!" said Pellicola. "Let's be on our way then."

The boys squatted down, Pasquale at the head of the stretcher, Giorgio at its foot, and grasped the handles.

"Wait!" Signora Assaroti took off her shawl and draped it over the mummy. "If a woman with child looks upon this horror, she might give birth to a monstrosity."

"Good thinking!" the doctor said. "Such things have been known to happen." To the apprentices he said, "You know where my house is—down the Via Filippo Ugolini, across the bridge, and through the old Porta Celle. Just knock on the door and my housekeeper will direct you to my laboratory. The Prior and I must stop off at the tobacconist's; we'll be along shortly. Careful. Bits of him might be inclined to fall off and we wouldn't want dogs making off with them."

"Or rats," agreed Giorgio, nodding sagely.

When the three of us arrived at the doctor's house, the boys carefully lowered the stretcher to the ground and knocked twice on the heavy wooden door. This was eventually opened by Isabella. "And what is that?" She pointed to the shawl-draped object on the stretcher.

"It's a mummy!" Pasquale replied and obligingly drew back a portion of his mother's shawl, revealing the mummy's hideous face.

The housekeeper squeaked once, very shrilly, and fainted dead away, just in time for the arrival of the doctor, his cousin, and the Prior, all three of whom were smoking big cigars.

"Not again!" the doctor sighed. Kneeling, he reached into his breast pocket for a vial of smelling salts, which he uncorked and passed under the housekeeper's nose, causing her to sneeze and start. "Up you go." He took hold of her forearms and hauled her immense pile to her feet, where she wavered and swayed. "There now. Are you all right?"

"First *his* leg!" Isabella glared accusingly at Pepe. "Now this horror! Are you trying to frighten me to death?"

"Not at all, dear Isabella! We only seek to expand the frontiers of science."

"And where do you intend to do that?" the housekeeper demanded. "Not anywhere I need to dust, I hope!"

"Don't concern yourself. We're taking it out back to my laboratory. You shall never have to lay eyes upon it again."

"If you gentlemen will excuse me," Pepe said brightly, "I would like to visit with my leg now."

"His *leg!*" complained Isabella, looking bilious. "His *leg!*"

"Now, Isabella," the doctor reminded her. "He's not asking *you* to visit his leg!" He turned to Giorgio and Pasquale. "Let's go, boys."

"But we want to see the leg," they protested.

"You will. Rest assured," replied the doctor. "After you've safely transported our friend to the laboratory."

With that, we went our separate ways—Isabella, in a certain amount of high dudgeon, toward the kitchen, and the doctor, Cesare, the boys, and the mummy through to the back of the house and the stairs that led down into the garden. Pepe and I were alone in the shady corridor. "So, are you ready to see my leg?" he asked, rubbing his hands together in happy anticipation.

"I am."

"Delightful! It so loves visitors. It gets very lonely without the rest of me. Well, then. Come along."

Filled with equal parts excitement and trepidation, I followed a few steps behind the one-legged man as he hauled himself painfully up the stairs and lurched down the sloping hallway. He opened the door to his room with a flourish to reveal a large glass jar in which the lower portion of a leg amputated from just below the knee floated. The jar was set upon a small table before a fireplace and filled with a cloudy amber-colored liquid. The glass was smudged with fingerprints, presumably Pepe's own, made as he hung onto the jar, staring, staring at his dismembered limb with its splayed toes and ragged top—the amputation had not been a neat one. Pepe drew a chair up to the table, lowered himself into it, and leaning forward, wrapped his arms around the bottle. Pressing his nose to the glass, he whispered, "How are you? Yes, I know I haven't visited for a while. I've been away. Yes, of course. I've missed you too."

I stood awkwardly in the door, not knowing how I was supposed to behave in such a situation. It felt as though I was intruding on an intensely private moment—a tender scene between a man and a cherished part of him—surely not intended for public consumption.

Pepe remembered he had company. "Come, girl! Draw close! Have a good look! It doesn't bite. It has no teeth, as you can see."

I swallowed and crossed the short distance to the table. I bent down and peered into the cloudy liquid. The leg was pulsating ever so slightly. As you can imagine, this was unnerving. "Is it…it isn't…moving, is it?"

"It is!"

"But how…how can it do that?"

"I have no idea. I just know that it does. It beats like a heart. Put your hand on the glass."

I did and, sure enough, I could feel a vibration in the glass. It felt like a pulse. Quickly I withdrew my hand.

"Do you want to know something even stranger? It beats in rhythm with my own heart. I'll show you. Put one hand on my chest and one on the jar and you will see."

I did as he suggested and found that he was correct. The vibration through the glass kept pace with the beating of his heart. I hurriedly withdrew my hands and wiped them on my skirt.

"Do you want to know something else that is strange?" he asked dreamily. "I can still feel my leg. It's as if it's still attached to me. Every once in a while, I have a charley horse or a toe cramp and I feel it in that leg. What's more, if I happen to be around the jar at the time of that charley horse or toe cramp, the calf of my leg will knot up in a spasm or my toe will jerk. You can actually watch it happen."

By this time, he was making me extremely uncomfortable. "I...I'd better find the others," I said hurriedly. "Thank you very much, though, you know...for letting me see your leg." I fled to the hallway and retraced my steps to the foyer below. From there I headed in the direction I had seen the others go, through the house and down into the vast medicinal garden that lay between it and the river.

When I arrived at the laboratory at the garden's far end, the boys had just finished transferring the mummy from the stretcher to a marble-topped examination table.

"What was it like?" Pasquale asked me. "The leg, I mean."

Giorgio snorted stupidly. "I bet it made you swoon!"

"Nonsense!" I said. "I've helped to birth goats and lambs. My stomach is strong."

"She's from the country," Pasquale explained.

Dr. Pellicola turned away from the examining table. "Ah! Here you are, Signorina Mari! Well! What did you think of Pepe's leg?"

Not wishing to offend him, I replied, "It was very...it was interesting."

"It is, isn't it?"

"Back to the chapel with you now, lads. Chop! Chop!" Cesare told the boys. "I want that entire floor dug up by Vespers."

"But you said we could see Signor Passalacqua's leg," Pasquale protested.

"After you see Signor Passalacqua's leg then but be quick about it. No loitering."

"I wonder if you would be so kind as to perform a small service for us before you leave," Dr. Pellicola said to me. "Would you mind terribly fetching us a bottle of grappa? Isabella refuses to set foot out here and, besides, one hates to make the poor old thing walk such a long way with her bad hip."

"She hates me," Cesare said. "That's the reason she won't come."

"Stuff and nonsense, Bacigalupo," the doctor corrected him. "It's the dead things she can't stand. She has no stomach for them."

"Or me," Cesare persisted.

"I'll do it gladly," I said, welcoming the chance to have a better gander at the mummy.

Pellicola beamed. "There's a girl! Just ask Isabella."

I found the housekeeper crashing about the kitchen, muttering aloud to herself about it being unnatural to fawn over pieces of oneself no longer attached to one's body. "And what do you want?" she demanded.

"The doctor would like some grappa."

"Oh, he would, would he?"

"He sent me to fetch it."

She snorted and pointed to a cabinet. "I tell you, I cannot fathom how in Heaven's name he can expect me to continue in his employ when he is forever bringing dead things home! He's like a cat! Like a cat that brings you dead mice and ravaged birds and expects you to be thrilled about the whole thing! And now this…a *mummy!* Well, I'm *not* thrilled!"

I returned to the laboratory with the bottle of grappa. The doctor and Cesare were standing on either side of the examination table, gazing intently down at the mummy. "Ah, here she is!" cried Pellicola. "To the rescue!" He relieved me of the bottle. "Care for any yourself, my dear?" I shook my head. "Very wise. It would stunt your growth and that would be a shame. You're far too short as it is." He crossed over to a cabinet from which he procured two glasses, opened the bottle, poured two shots, handed one to Cesare and raised his glass. "To our mysterious friend!"

"Our mysterious friend!" Cesare said. The two men tapped glasses and raised them. In the meantime, I commandeered a tall stool, situated it in such a way that it provided me with a good view of the mummy, and clambered up on it.

"Another?" asked the doctor.

"Please."

The doctor poured; the men drank, then returned their attention to the mummy.

"What's that around his neck?" Cesare pointed to a frayed fibrous tube encircling the mummy's papery throat—easy to miss, being the same general color and texture as the rest of the mummy.

The doctor leaned in for a closer look. "I say! Good eye, Bacigalupo! That's rope, if I'm not mistaken. Maybe our friend was executed by hanging."

Cesare shook his head. "I don't think so. You can't bury a convicted felon or a suicide in sacred ground."

"How do you explain the rope then?"

Cesare pondered this. "Maybe he was dragged about by means of it. The way prisoners are. Or slaves."

"But how did he die?"

"Surely the more important question is: How did he become a mummy? We all die sooner or later, but very few of us go on to become mummies."

"Good point! But let's sit, shall we?" The doctor gestured toward a small, round table and four chairs positioned under a large bay window overlooking the rapids. "All this excitement! It's left me somewhat fatigued."

"Me too," said Cesare.

"What about you, Signorina Mari? Will you sit?"

"I am content to remain as I am," I replied.

The two men retired to the table and the doctor poured another couple of shots. "Since this isn't Egypt, I'd wager our mummy is a natural rather than an artificial one. Probably his bodily fluids were so rapidly absorbed by mold present in the soil where he was buried that he dehydrated before he could properly decompose. I'd put my money on *Hippa Bombicina Pers*, a mold found in abundance in this region. You've seen it, Bacigalupo—those white flakes in the soil when you turn it with a shovel."

"Interesting! Hippa Bomba…. Whatever! Dehydrated?" said Cesare. "I say, Pellicola, could I have another grappa? I am so excited about our dehydrated friend here that I am quite beside myself! After all, it's not every day one finds a mummy!"

"Indeed!" The doctor poured two more shots.

Cesare raised his glass." To the dead!"

"To the dead! Long may they continue thus!"

"I think that goes without saying!"

"But continue with your…you know…your discourse." Cesare was slurring his words a little now. "You were speaking of…natural mummies. What causes them. Mold. That was it. Yup. A fascinating topic! Continue, sir!"

But the doctor had sagged into a kind of reverie, his head lolling to one side, a silver spindle of drool beginning to spiral its way down his chin from the corner of his gaping mouth.

"Pellicola!" Cesare managed. "You're drifting!"

"What?" The doctor rallied himself, blinking. "Ah, yes. Mummies. Mold. Dehydration…" He too, was beginning to slur his words. "And what about Naples?"

"What about it?"

"In Naples, they bury their dead without coffins. Do you know why?"

"No."

"Because of the volcano!"

"Monte Vesuvio?"

"The same!"

"The Neapolitans just *hurl* their dead into Monte Vesuvio?"

"No! Of course not!" Pellicola corrected him. "That would be cremation. In Naples, there's a high percentage of volcanic ash in the soil—very dehydrating, volcanic ash! So, the Neapolitans bury their dead, then, after a year or so, they dig them up—all dried out and perfectly preserved—and put them in above-ground vaults."

"A sensible people, the Neapolitans. To the Neapolitans!" Cesare raised his glass, then squinted at it. "Is this empty? I can't focus."

"It is!" said Pellicola. He filled it. "To the Neapolitans!"

"To the Neapolitans!"

The two men sat for a moment, staring straight ahead, weaving to the extent that that was possible, given their seated position.

Then, "I say, Bacigalupo, is your glass empty?"

Bacigalupo held his glass at arm's length and squinted at it. "So it would appear!"

"Girl! Where is that girl?" Pellicola muttered. "She was here just a minute ago."

"I'm right here," I told him.

The doctor stared at me; he was having trouble focusing. "So you are! Had me worried there for a moment. We need some more grappa."

I glanced at the bottle. It was empty. "There's no more," I told him. "You drank it all."

"No more? Nonsense! There's always more. Off to the kitchen with you now. Straightaway! Tell that old biddy Isabella we need another bottle."

I dismounted from the stool, returned to the house and fetched a fresh bottle of grappa. I arrived back at the laboratory to find the doctor relieving himself into a boxwood hedge just outside the door. I averted my eyes until he was finished and waited while he wobbled back inside before reentering the laboratory myself. "Ah, it's you!" he greeted me. "What took you so long?"

I handed him the bottle. He poured Cesare and himself another glass and raised it. "To…who? What? Who are we toasting?"

"To whoever the mummy was in life!" Cesare suggested.

"To you! Whoever you were, you sorry specimen! You miserable wretch!"

"How do you know he was a miserable wretch?" Cesare wondered. "Maybe he was a happy man, prosperous, with a large and loving family."

The doctor sniggered, hiccupped, and managed, "I doubt it!" before placing his elbows on the table and laying his right cheek on his forearms. His eyes slid shut.

"What? Pellicola? Are you asleep?"

The doctor mumbled something incoherent.

"Oh, very well then! If you're going to be that way." And Cesare too, set his elbows on the table and slumped forward, his forehead resting on the back of his hands.

I walked over to the examination table and stared down at the mummy—at the brittle leather of its skin, the yawning eye sockets, the howl frozen on its twisted face, the mop of matted hair atop its head. "Who are you?" I whispered. "Who are you and what's your story?"

No reply.

I left the laboratory, closing the door quietly behind me so as not to wake Cesare and Pellicola. As I made my way through the herb garden, I encountered Pepe coming the other way, carrying a battered looking saddle.

"Are you going out riding?" I asked.

"Perhaps," he replied. "But first I want to look in on my cousin and his newest acquisition."

"They drank too much grappa and fell asleep," I told him. "Best let them sleep it off."

"Oh, I wouldn't dream of disturbing them," Pepe assured me. "I can be very quiet. Very quiet, indeed! I just want to have a peek at our new friend. Just a peek."

I shrugged. "Do as you like."

Pepe smiled. His scar was shiny and dappled, like abalone, and his teeth were a peculiar shade of green. "I always do."

Cesare returned to the house for dinner, rumpled and dazed. He reported that the mummy discovered earlier that day had vanished from the laboratory as he and the doctor napped. So, coincidently, had Pepe.

"I saw him," I said. "We crossed paths in the doctor's garden. He said he wanted to take a peek at the mummy."

"I expect that villain stole it then," said Antonella, ladling thick stew into bowls and sounding faintly triumphant. "He probably intends to sell it. And a pretty penny he'll make, too, now that's it's in such short supply."

"Sell it?" I asked. "To whom? For what?"

"An apothecary, of course. For mummia!" Then, at the blank look on my face, "Don't tell me you've never heard of mummia?"

"Now, Antonella! Mari can't help it if she is a little backward. Country folk always are." He attempted to take her hand, but she snatched it away. "Sit down, dearest," he pleaded. "You will have to get used to it, you know, once we are married."

"And until that sad day, I will eat my meals in the kitchen, like the poor relation I am!" Antonella proclaimed. In proof of which point, she retreated to the kitchen; she did not, however, close the door to the dining room.

Cesare sighed and rubbed his forehead. "Mummia is mummy flesh," he told me. "Fantastic stuff, really. It's used to restore wasted limbs and to treat heckticks. It even cures ulcers and corruptions."

"What are heckticks?" I asked.

"The fidgets," Antonella answered from the kitchen.

I was intrigued. "Mummy flesh is a medicine with specific applications? Like foxglove for dropsy or mugwort for arthritis? What a concept! And how do you administer it? Do you...eat it?"

"Sometimes, but mostly it's applied topically," said Cesare. "An apothecary will process it into tinctures, elixir, treacle, and balsams, then use it to treat patients. It's terribly rare right now, the imports from Egypt having recently dried up."

"Your mummy will fetch a good price. That's for sure," observed Antonella. "And Signor Passalacqua will drink and gamble it all away in no time!"

"Look, Antonella, it's ridiculous for you to be in the other room if you're going to continue to talk to us!" Cesare objected.

I poked around in my stew; it was a uniform brown color and very glutinous. Antonella was not a very good cook. "Is there one of those…what do you call it…the person who makes the medicine…is there such a person in Casteldurante?"

"An apothecary?" said Cesare. "Why, yes. There are two, in fact—Giovanni Bertoldi and…ummm?"

"Alphonso Lanza," Antonella supplied the name.

"Well, why don't you check with them and see if Signor Passalacqua has approached them?"

Antonella snorted. "Hah! As if that would work!"

"I'm afraid she's right," Cesare agreed. "Pepe is not so stupid as that. No, he would have spirited it out of town most likely—to Urbino or Fossembrone perhaps."

"But how would he get there?" Antonella wondered. "With a mummy in tow?"

I remembered the saddle. "On horseback. When I saw him he was carrying a saddle."

"Well, that's that then!" said Cesare glumly. "He's gone and won't be back until he runs out of money. Pellicola is a brilliant fellow, but he has a real blind spot when it comes to his cousin. He thinks that Pepe can do no wrong and cannot be convinced otherwise. Too bad. I was thinking of having a glass cabinet made so that we might properly exhibit our mummy."

"And where did you think you were going to put that case?" demanded Antonella. "Not in my house, I hope!"

"In the Capella Cola, my dear, in the chapel! Will you please come and sit down with us, Antonella? Please!"

"I'm not saying another word!"

That night, I described the events of the day to Lady Sibylla.

"That priest knows something and I'm just the one to make him talk!" she declared.

"But how, Milady? How can you possibly do that?"

"He's the one who likes mugwort, and your mother sent a big bag of mugwort down with me and that appalling cheese. It's probably still in the satchel. Tell his housekeeper that your mother sent it for him and you'd like to give it to him."

"And then?"

"You take me along with you in the satchel. When we get him alone, I will speak to him."

"How?"

"The same way I am speaking to you now. You know that thing I do when I sound like I'm everywhere and nowhere at the same time? I'll do that. Trust me, Mariuccia Umbellino. The priest's a superstitious man. He won't doubt that I am who I say I am. I'll give him such a fright that he'll spill the beans."

The following morning, Padre Eusebio woke with a start. Someone was knocking on his door. No. Not knocking. Pounding.

"What? Who? What is it?" was all he could manage. His brain was still tangled up in dreams. Terrifying dreams. That the body had been found. Finally found after all these years.

"It's Caterina Assaroti," came the reply through the door. "You have visitors."

"At this hour of the morning?"

"It's ten o'clock, Padre!"

"I'm sick! I ache all over. Tell them to go away."

"That's just it, Padre. It's Signorina Umbellino. She's brought you mugwort. For your arthritis."

"Ooooh," said Padre Eusebio. On the one hand, he couldn't bear to see another human soul, not until he wrapped his mind around exactly what had happened the previous day—for some reason he was having difficulty remembering just what that was.

On the other hand, the relief that mugwort would bring him was sorely tempting. "Oh, all right." Everything will be all right, he told himself, as long as nobody digs up the floor of the chapel. Then he remembered. Someone had. Someone had dug up the floor of the chapel and the body had been found! "Oh, my stars!" he whispered, shrinking beneath his bedcovers as the door opened and Signora Assaroti ushered me into the dark bedroom, saying, "I will leave you to find your own way out. I'm off to market."

"Take your time," I said, retrieving a chair from beside the window and repositioning it at the old man's bedside. I sat down, the satchel on my lap. "I understand you're not feeling well."

"When have I ever felt well?" complained the old priest. "If there was a time, I can't remember it. Old age is a terrible burden. Die young. That's my advice."

"Mama sent you down some mugwort. I'd forgotten about it until last night when I was going through the satchel she sent. It should relieve your suffering a little."

"A great kindness—"

I cut him off. "First we talk," I said, "about what happened yesterday."

"About what? What happened? I can't remember. My memory," he tittered. "It's going, you know."

"But I imagine you remember what happened before that?" Lady Sibylla spoke; her voice sounded as though it was coming from all directions at once, crystal clear and not quite human. "At my grotto."

Eusebio's watery eyes opened wide. He shrank into the bedclothes. "Who is that?"

"Who do you think it is?"

The old man looked wildly around the room. "Show yourself!"

"I cannot be seen. I am none the less here."

"The witch? Is it the witch?"

Lady Sibylla was indignant. "What? A witch? Is that what you think I am? No, you wretch, I am not a witch. I am a Speaking Virgin—one of the only four Speaking Virgins that the world has ever known! At least, last time I checked."

"How did you come to be here?" he cried.

"Too many questions!"

"I'm sorry!" He cowered in his bed. "He made me do it! My Bishop. The Prior, too. They don't understand that there are rules that cannot be broken, lines that cannot be crossed. They don't understand that you have been there since the beginning. I know. My mother taught me. The Bishop's to blame. If you want to punish anyone, punish him!"

"You wish me to spare you?" Sibylla asked.

"Yes, oh, please, yes!"

"Then you must tell us about the body—the body found under the floor of your little chapel. You do know I caused the earth tremor that tumbled your decrepit little clerestory, don't you? Not my finest work, but I'm a little rusty."

"You caused the earth tremor?" creaked Eusebio.

"Mama did warn the Prior," I reminded him. "He didn't listen."

"I can do worse, now that I'm warmed up. Don't be a fool, old man. Tell us what you know, or I'll open up a sinkhole under that bed and send you straight to Hades."

"All right! All right! I'll tell you! But I'm an old man and don't remember so well and, in any case, you're making me very nervous!"

"Take a deep breath," I instructed him. "Now let it out slowly. One. Two. Three."

After a few such calming breaths Padre Eusebio cleared his throat and, in a halting voice, told the following tale.

Padre Eusebio heard confessions on Wednesdays after Vespers. Not that many people actually confessed to Padre Eusebio. Most people went to the Duomo or to San Francesco. Eusebio found this arrangement entirely to his liking; it meant that he wasn't forced to listen to anyone's tedious prattling and he could go home early.

Nevertheless, to maintain appearances, Eusebio showed up, as always, at the posted hour and took his place on the appropriate side of the grille with the intention of remaining there for a quarter of an hour, no more, no less. During this time, he usually trimmed his nails, humming, or nibbled on a plate of biscuits, or closed his eyes and, leaning the side of his head against the wooden wall of the confessional, napped.

On this particular Wednesday, however, he stewed. Just the week before, Adeodatus's predecessor as Bishop, Prospero Sordello, had humiliated him in front of all of Casteldurante by setting him up to play the fool. Knowing full well that the old priest's toenails were sorely afflicted with fungus and that his feet exuded an unpleasant, yeasty odor, Prospero had nevertheless insisted upon him being one of three priests whose feet he would ceremonially wash at the service on Holy Thursday. Then, when it actually came time for him to perform this ritual in front of the entire congregation, Prospero knelt before him, took one look at his feet and pretended to gag before crying out, "What have we here, Father? Hooves? Are you the Devil then?" The other two priests on the dais erupted in laughter, followed by the entire congregation. "Ha! Ha! Ha!" they roared. "Good one, Bishop!"

For a dreadful moment it had seemed to Eusebio that

he was utterly paralyzed. A darkness passed before his eyes, accompanied by a lurch in his stomach that sent bile surging up his throat. A second later up came his dinner (a lumpy repast of polenta and chunks of fish), a good deal of which sprayed the lower portion of Prospero's chasuble. Eusebio staggered to his much-maligned feet, tumbled off the dais, and exited the Duomo by its side door, propelled forward on rolling swells of laughter from the congregation.

The recollection of this recent humiliation had so consumed him that Wednesday in the confessional that he failed to notice when a penitent inconveniently slipped into its other compartment. "Hello!" said the person after a moment. "Is anyone there?"

Eusebio pulled himself together and reluctantly slid open the grille. "What is it, my son?"

"I have come to confess my sins, Father."

"Well, I didn't think you had come to sell me a goat! What is it you wish to confess? And, if you don't mind, could you be quick about it? My dinner is getting cold and I'm in a very bad mood."

"Bless me, Father, for I have sinned—"

The priest interrupted him. "Don't you want to know why I am in a bad mood?"

"Not really."

"That says it all, doesn't it?" Eusebio fumed. "You don't care about me, but I'm supposed to care about you. I get it. Go on. Continue. But be brief, I beg you. God knows what you have done. I don't need the details."

There was a pause, then, "It is not what I have done so much as what I am about to do."

"There's no point confessing to sins you have yet to commit."

"Why not?"

"Because it doesn't count."

"Why not?"

"Because it doesn't work that way. You can't confess *in advance*, because you can't feel genuine remorse in advance. You can only imagine that you will feel remorse. And that's not good enough."

"What about Indulgences?"

"What about them?"

"You can purchase Indulgences in advance to reduce the amount of time you have to spend in Purgatory."

"Ah, but that's different. That's advance planning."

"And repenting in advance isn't?"

"Yes, but with Indulgences, actual money exchanges hands," Eusebio pointed out. "That's the difference. It's a big difference."

"Let me get this straight," said the penitent. "If I pay you, you'll absolve me for sins I have yet to commit?"

Eusebio entertained the notion for a moment, then thought better of it. What if Prospero learned that he had accepted money for absolution? Not that the bishop would think it was a bad idea. He would probably think it a good idea. He would just be peeved that the penitent had not come to *him*. And who was to say that this was not a setup, that Prospero had not put this man up to this to frame him? After all, the bishop was clearly out to get him. "I can't do that," he told the penitent. "I tell you what. Go commit your sin. Come back next Wednesday at this time. Confess, and I'll absolve you. That's the way the system works. Now, if you are quite through…?" And he made as if to close the grille.

"But I can't come back next Wednesday!" the penitent protested.

"Why not?" The priest was losing what little patience he had. "Are you traveling to another town? Are you moving to Austria or Moldavia? In that case, make confession to whatever priest there is to be found. My feelings will not be hurt."

"I won't be able to confess because…well…because I'll be dead."

"Dead? What are you talking about? Dead? How do you know you will be dead? Do you have a fatal illness?"

"No. The truth is…well, the truth is I plan to kill myself. Very shortly. Within the week."

"You plan to take your own life?" Eusebio asked.

"Yes."

"Suicide?"

"That's right."

"You realize that suicide is a mortal sin?"

"I do," replied the petitioner. "That's the reason I'm here. Because I'm about to commit a mortal sin and I need absolution."

"You do realize that you're going to Hell?" Eusebio asked. "Because you are. No two ways about it."

"Actually, I'm rather hoping for Purgatory."

"Impossible. Suicides go to Hell. Everyone knows that!"

"I'm hoping to negotiate my position."

"With whom? With God?" Eusebio snorted. "Good luck with that!" Once again he made as if to close the grille.

"No, Father, wait!" the petitioner pled. "Just a minute,

I beg of you. For you see, I am not like other men and, this being the case, can I not hope to be treated differently?"

Eusebio frowned. "How are you not like other men?"

"I have a condition. A rare condition. I...well, I'm a jettatore."

Eusebio was struck dumb. A jettatore? Someone who, without wishing it, casts the evil eye on whatever happens to be the object of his gaze? Eusebio understood that such unfortunate beings existed—just as giants and other freaks of nature did—but he had certainly never encountered one.

"Father? Are you all right?"

"Yes. I mean. You aren't by any chance *looking* at me, are you? Because my health is delicate at the best of times."

"Never fear," the penitent assured him. "I am wearing an eye patch. Would you care to hear my story? Then you might have more compassion for me."

"I doubt that!" Eusebio replied. "But go ahead. It's bound to be interesting."

"Interesting, but tragic," the penitent agreed. He cleared his throat and began: "After I had inadvertently caused my poor mother to sicken and die within a week of my birth, my nonna took me in, much against the wishes of our fellow villagers, I might add. She was a wise woman—some said a witch. She diagnosed my condition immediately and fashioned a patch for me that covered my offending eye, as a result of which I lived. Oh, but that she had not!"

"I don't understand. As long as your eye remains covered, what's the problem?"

"People would not let me be. They would not tolerate me living among them. When my nonna died, the villagers turned on me and drove me from my home near San Sisto. I was just fourteen at the time, but resilient and resourceful beyond my years. My affliction compelled me to be. I traveled to a town in Umbria—Madonnuccia it was called, near Sansepulcro. There, a kind old tinker taught me his trade and I lived with him and his wife for five years. Then, one night, while I was sleeping, he tugged ever so gently at my eye patch to see what it concealed (he was as curious as a cat, old Pietro). But he did not tug gently enough. Startled (for, as you can imagine, I am a light sleeper), I opened my eye and the old man's fate was sealed. He became very ill with diarrhea and died within the week, leaving me his tools. While he was ill, however, and delirious, he revealed my secret to his wife, who told the entire town. Again I was forced to flee. This same story has repeated itself time and time again throughout the last twenty years. After the first few attempts at settling someplace, I gave up. Instead, I became a traveling tinker, moving from village to village, leaving before anyone discovered my terrible secret. Sometimes I did not leave in time and then there were consequences. This then has been the sad story of my life, Padre. No friends. No family. No place to call home. The constant danger that I will harm innocent creatures. As you might imagine I am sick to death of the whole thing."

"I can see your point," reflected Padre Eusebio. "Still, to kill yourself…"

"I did not make myself this way. God did. The way I see it, He owes me."

"Hush! He might hear you!"

"And do what to me? How could He make my life any more miserable than it already is?"

Eusebio considered this. "He could give you boils," he suggested.

"Just do me this small kindness, Father: Forgive me for the sin I am about to commit. After all, what skin is it off your nose?"

"A great deal of skin!" Eusebio retorted. "If I do what you ask, I endanger my own soul, and for what? Unless... unless..."

As he was speaking, an idea had occurred to him, inchoate as yet and shapeless as a squall, but it involved Prospero and, therefore, interested him greatly—as all things having to do with his new archenemy did.

"Unless what?" the tinker asked.

"I'm thinking!"

If he could get the tinker to cast his Evil Eye on Prospero, then.... Then what? All his problems would be solved! But how to persuade him? How? His disinclination to harm others was clear.

"If you want money..." the tinker began.

"Money? No, I don't want money! But there is one thing you could do for me."

"And what is that?"

"You could cast your Evil Eye on my enemy."

The tinker was shocked. "You're asking me to deliberately and knowingly harm another human being? Something I've spent my entire life trying to avoid!"

"I didn't say you'd like it."

"Well, I don't!"

"Fine! That's the deal. Absolution for assassination. Take it or leave it."

"I'll leave it, thank you very much!"

"All right, then. We're through here. Go away. Scoot and good riddance!" Again Eusebio reached for the grille.

"No, wait! Don't leave!" the tinker pleaded. "Tell me about him. Your enemy. Is he a wicked man?"

"He's a jackal," Eusebio replied. "A hyena."

"He's a criminal then? A murderer? Perhaps a rapist?"

"Well, he's been very unpleasant to me if that's what you're asking."

"He's beaten you? Robbed you? Tortured you?"

"In a manner of speaking. Details are unimportant."

"But he is a villain, deserving of death?"

"Of course," Eusebio replied. "Would I ask you to curse him if he were not a villain? What do you take me for?"

The tinker sighed deeply. "Where can I find him?"

Eusebio's heart did a little jig. "In the Duomo."

This surprised the tinker. "What's he doing in the Duomo?"

"Saying Mass."

"He's a priest?"

"Actually, he's the bishop. You'll recognize him by the outfit. You know. Crozier. Mitre."

"Are you crazy?" the tinker demanded. "I can't cast the mal'occhio on a bishop!"

"Why not?"

"Because!"

"Because why?"

"Because he's a bishop! That's why! Think about it!"

Eusebio snorted. "I have thought about it! Obviously! And I see nothing wrong with it. A man of the cloth can

be as wicked as the next man! The Pope comes to mind!"
Despite his bravado he saw that he was losing the tinker.
He had to come up with something else he could offer him.
Something to sweeten the pot. "Just how is it that you plan
to kill yourself?"

"Why?"

"Just curious."

"Hanging, I think."

"Messy," said Eusebio. "Are you sure you wouldn't rather
poison yourself? Although, come to think of it, that's messy
too. All that vomiting and rolling about in agony."

"I've settled on hanging."

"And where exactly had you planned on doing this?"

"Just outside the wall of the cemetery of San Vivaldo.
There's a very tall oak with a sturdy branch that is at least
twelve feet from the ground. It should do nicely."

"Near San Vivaldo, eh? That's rather ironic, don't you
think?"

"What do you mean?"

"Think about it. As a suicide you can't be buried in hal-
lowed ground. So, you hang yourself just outside the wall of
the cemetery and there you will remain for eternity—separated from God's love by the wall of sin. Sure, I can absolve
you in advance of your sin, but your body...that must lie
forever beyond the pale. Unless…"

"Unless what?"

"Unless you modify your plan."

"In what way?"

"You wait. You hang yourself here, in the Cappella, rather
than outside the cemetery. There's quite the drop from the

corbel that extends out from the choir. All you would have to do is to climb the stairs to the choir, fasten one end of your rope to the corbel and the noose around your neck and jump. Your neck would snap instantly. No struggle. No pain. You could do this at night, when no one is here. Of course I would know the plan, be in on it, as it were, but I couldn't be here. Much too upsetting. Not that I am fond of you or anything. Just...death." Eusebio shuddered. "Worrisome. Then, later on that night or early in the morning, I could creep in, cut you down and bury you in one of the empty vaults behind the altar. That way you would be absolved, buried in holy ground, and no one but you and I would know about it."

"That's brilliant!"

"Of course, all this is predicated on your doing what I want," Eusebio reminded him. "Which is to say—"

"That I cast the mal'occhio on the bishop."

"Exactly."

This time the tinker considered the proposition for only a matter of moments. "All right," he said. "You drive a hard bargain and, in the end, it's too good a deal to pass up. Count me in."

"Excellent!" declared Eusebio. "Now you go away and look at the bishop. If he falls grievously ill, or, better yet, dies, then come to me straightaway and I shall absolve you in advance of the sin of suicide and we will carry out the rest of our plan that very night."

And so it was that, following hard on the heels of the four o'clock Mass on the Monday after Easter, 1784, Bishop Prospero Sordello complained of a stomach ache and gas pains. He described these to his entourage as feeling like, "rats gnawing at my entrails" before collapsing in a heap of clerical trappings in the foyer of the Episcopal Palace. It required four men to get him to his feet and then manhandle him upstairs; the bishop was a big man and unwieldy as a mattress. No sooner had they heaved him into his bed than the vomiting, at times projectile, began, then the diarrhea. The physician was called for, but apart from applying a few leeches to the bishop's chest in the brief intervals between spew, could only surmise from the suddenness and severity of the symptoms that the bishop had eaten a bad sausage—a very bad sausage. The following Sunday, Eusebio's nemesis was lying in state in the Duomo amid much lamentation on the part of the congregation as a whole and just a little well-masked jubilation on the part of the priest of Cappella di Cola.

That same evening, the tinker confessed to Padre Eusebio in advance for his suicide and Eusebio granted him absolution. Eusebio than returned to the rectory, leaving the tinker to climb the stairs to the little choir and hang himself from the corbel. Just before midnight, Padre Eusebio returned to his little church, cut the tinker down, and, with much effort and a great deal of cursing (for, as it turned out, the tinker was a tall, ungainly man and difficult for the diminutive priest to manage), he dragged him the length of the Cappella and bumped him up the steps leading to the altar. He lifted up the floor tiles and stuffed the tinker's body into one of the vaults previously occupied by a corpse that had, in his predecessor's time, been disinterred and moved to the cemetery of San Vivaldo in compliance with the Edict of St. Cloud.

Eusbeio was a bit worried that the stink of a rotting

corpse might alert someone to the tinker's interment behind the altar. To his relief, there was no perceptible odor. This was because the mold that dehydrated the body and turned it into a mummy did so in a remarkably efficient and swift manner. That concern having been assuaged, Eusebio figured that, as long as no one dug up the chapel floor and found the tinker's body, his secret would be safe.

"That's it," the old priest concluded. "That's my story. What are you going to do to me? Are you going to tell Adeodatus? Because if you tell Adeodatus, my goose is cooked. You might as well kill me now if you're intent upon telling Adeodatus, but could you do it in the least painful way possible? That's all I ask. On second thought, why not let me live? All of this happened a very long time ago."

I ignored all these questions, asking instead, "What was the tinker's name?"

Eusebio was taken aback. "His name? Why do you want to know his name?"

"Was it Enzo?"

"I don't know. Maybe."

"You're thinking what I'm thinking, aren't you?" Lady Sibylla asked me.

"As in how many jettatore tinkers can there have been wandering around Umbria and the Marches at that time?" I asked.

"Exactly!"

"So the tinker who curdled Padre Antonio's eyes—Enzo the Tinker—he's the mummy!"

"You knew this fellow?" Padre Eusebio asked.

"Oh, yes," I said. "He stayed awhile in Montemonaco years and years ago when my parents were children. He was forced to flee when a boy tore off his eye patch on a dare and was blinded. That boy grew up to be the village priest."

"The one who pantomimes the Mass because he can't read?"

"The same!"

"Well, I never!"

"It's a small world!" exclaimed the Oracle and everyone agreed.

"So, what about me?" Eusebio asked. "Are you going to tell the Bishop?"

"If you don't tell on me, I'll not tell on you," the Oracle assured him. "Otherwise…"

"Oh, I can keep a secret!" Eusebio declared. "I can be most devious!"

"Clearly."

"All right then," I said. I stood and turned toward the door.

"Uh-hem. Aren't you forgetting something?" Eusebio asked.

"What?" I asked.

"The mugwort." And he tilted back his head and flared his nostrils.

The following day, I prevailed upon Cesare to dispatch Pasquale by stagecoach and then by donkey to Montemonaco, bearing with him the satchel containing Sibylla's jug. The Oracle had had her first outing in more than a millennium; it had been a success, but it was time for her to return to Monte Vettore, and besides, I wasn't sure how much longer I could keep her under wraps. I stayed behind in Casteldurante to care for Cico, who continued to be a clingy, fussy infant whom only I could settle.

Cesare finally talked Antonella into marrying him in May of that year. After that, the entire household headed south along the coast to Martinsicuro, then inland. When our coach arrived at Ascoli Piceno, my father met us, and we parted ways—Cesare and Antonella continued on to the Terme Aquasancta where they would take the waters and fight over every single thing while Cico and I traveled on to Montemonaco with Papa.

Our arrival coincided with a great occasion. For the past several months the men of the village had been hard at work excavating the entrance to the grotto just beyond and beneath the one formerly inhabited by the Sibyl. This was a hugely tall cavern as big as a piazza. Because the stalactites and stalagmites that glowed and sparkled in the light pouring through a sinkhole in the mountain's flank looked as though a mad confectioner had swirled them into creation out of pink icing sugar, the men of the town decided to call the cavern *Il Grotto Rosato*—the Pink Grotto. It bristled with crystalline columns, jagged points and formations that, if one looked at them in a certain way, resembled angels or the Madonna or the altar of a church. A river slipped through the echoing cavern like a side-winding snake, a murmur of water, cold and thick.

That Sunday after Mass, the day of the installation, Padre Antonio Di Nardo organized a procession from the Church of Sant'Agata to the Grotto Rosato. Everyone in the village took part. Babies and small children were carried by their parents or older siblings and those of the elderly who could not walk were borne on stretchers. The procession began in the little square in front of the church and wound up through Montemonaco to our farm, where the Sibyl's jug was ceremoniously collected. As the person responsible for rescuing the Sibyl in the first place, Mama was given the honor of carrying her jug. Upon this occasion, the shortcut to the grotto via the goat path was not used. Instead, the procession made its way up the road and through the Gola dell'Infernaccia. After all, the whole point of a procession is to advance slowly, solemnly, and even laboriously. The best processions, as everyone knows, are those characterized by a certain amount of ardor, of staggering, of being certain that something of great value is about to be dropped, of relief when it is not.

When, at length, the procession had snaked through the narrow Gola to arrive at the newly dug out clearing, the Lamiae were waiting for us, a dozen serpents as long as a grown man's forearm, with jewels for eyes and sleek bodies brilliant with phosphorescence. It was Sunday, after all. Until the Pope said Mass on the following day, this was the shape the Oracle's handmaidens took. Who knows how these things get started? The Old Ones were as prone to transformations as the New Ones are to miracles.

At this juncture, torches were lit by which we could see to make our way down the ramp to the lower grotto. Needless to say, there was much exclaiming over the wondrous beauty and fantastical appearance of the cavern on the part of the women and children and old people—after all, this was our first glimpse of the Grotto Rosato, and for many it would be their only glimpse.

The strongest boy in the village bore a chair strapped to his back the entire way. It was the best chair in the village, made of oak with carved arms and upholstered in burgundy velvet, a little tatty with age. For as long as anyone could remember, it had resided throne-like and stiff in the vestry of the church. No one knew where it had come from, but it must have originated in one of the valley towns. There was not a chair like it anywhere on the mountain. It was the job of the Lamiae to determine the position of the chair. However, they could not make up their minds and grew so confused and excited at the prospect that they tied themselves into knots and began to shriek like peacocks. This, in turn, caused the children to shriek like peacocks. Finally, Padre Antonio intervened and arbitrarily picked a spot on the riverbank beneath a formation resembling a baldachin of translucent alabaster. Here the boy set the chair, upon which Mama placed the jug, and we Montemonaci bade a formal farewell to our Oracle.

We would never again descend into the grotto like this—in a group. Instead we would come alone or perhaps accompanied by one other, full of trepidation or grief stricken, to seek Lady Sibylla's advice or assistance. This was the way it had been for centuries; this was the way it would be henceforth.

Cico and I returned to Casteldurante a fortnight after the installation. My nephew was to be Cesare's only heir; Antonella would bear her husband no children. It was therefore Cico's destiny to be the "Son" in "Bacigalupo & Son" and, for that, he needed to reside in town. There were some in Casteldurante and in Montemonaco too, who thought I should marry, but there was no man who interested me in the slightest, and, as I grew older, the subject was gradually dropped.

Instead, I accompanied Cico on his trips to the factory—for he could not bear to be separated from me for any length of time, even as a young man—with the result that I ended up learning the majolica business as thoroughly as any man. Indeed, better.

This proved useful since Cesare dropped dead at the age of forty—as anyone could have predicted, for he had grown immensely fat—and I was compelled to take over the running of the business. Cico, though sweet, was a basket case for much of his short life. He died at the age of twenty-eight, but not without producing his own, single heir, yet another Cico, whom I also raised. All told, I have raised four Cicos. The one who fetched you from the convent, Padre…he is only the most recent. I am happy to say that, with each generation, the strength of the original love spell my mother cast on Cesare has waned a little. This latest Cico is inordinately, indeed, slavishly fond of me, but at least he doesn't constantly cling to me and whimper when I leave the room. At my great age, that would be too much to bear.

As for Antonella, she remained with me until her death some dozen years ago. Ours was not what you would call a close relationship. You see, I knew her secret while she knew none of mine. However, we tolerated one another well enough. It is a big house, after all.

So, speaking of secrets, there you have it, Father—mine. And now that I have told someone—someone who is pledged to keep my confidences to himself on pain of hellfire—I am going on a journey. It will not be as arduous a journey as it was in years past. We have trains now. However, let me tell you, any journey is momentous when you are ninety-nine years old. This Cico can manage without me, though I know he will be sad to see me go. Well, I would be going soon in any case, wouldn't I? I have it in my head to go back to Montemonaco, to Monte Vettore. I haven't spoken to the Oracle for such a long time. I would like to before I die.

That's all, Father. You can go. I'll see to it that Cico makes a little donation to the Convent. And, Father…tell no one of this. They wouldn't believe you if you did.

ACKNOWLEDGMENTS

I would like to acknowledge the ongoing support of the Ontario Arts Council for this project and others over many years. Thank you. Thanks also to my careful and insightful readers: Catherine Leggett, Pamela Rooks and Ken Trevenna.

ONTARIO ARTS COUNCIL
CONSEIL DES ARTS DE L'ONTARIO
an Ontario government agency
un organisme du gouvernement de l'Ontario

ABOUT THE AUTHOR

MELISSA HARDY has published five novels and two collections of short stories, including *Broken Road, The Uncharted Heart,* and *A Cry of Bees.* She has won the Journey Prize and been published in numerous journals, including *The Atlantic, Exile,* and *Descant.* Her short fiction has been widely anthologized, including twice in *Best American Short Stories* and in *The Year's Best Fantasy and Horror* and once in *Best Canadian Short Stories.* She has five children and two grandchildren and makes her home in Port Stanley, Ontario.